I0614691

SPY THRILLER

THE SLEEPER SERIES

WHO SPREADS FOR WHOM

By Anna Schlegel

BOOK TWO

Translation from Russian

Schlegel Press Association

Who Spreads for Whom by Anna Schlegel
Book Two of The Sleeper Series

Published by Schlegel Press Association
Friedrichstr. 123
Berlin, Germany 10117

ISBN: 9780998185385

First Edition: February 2017

Translated by Alla Koshechkina
Cover photography by Alamy & Fotolia

"...The Sleeper Series is a modern, fast-paced spin on British Intelligence operations that offers an entirely different perspective on why intelligence people become defectors."

- *MSNBC*

"...spy novel, promising to unravel the tangled web of a strange couple caught in the middle of an espionage game of British intelligence."

- *The Huffington Post*

"...a thriller that begins with a couple's discussion about intelligence processes and evolves to a cat-and-mouse game played out across the streets of Europe."

- *Midwest Book Review*

Also By Anna Schlegel

THE SLEEPER SERIES

MONEY CAN'T LIE

Book One of The Sleeper Series
Should there be three pieces of crap, this is of the British Intelligence classic.

THE GODS SMILE ON THE BASTARDS

Book Three of The Sleeper Series
Once you are able to see the intelligence's handwriting, you may see the words of failure inscribed in the same handwriting, telling of a failure they are yet unaware of.

ONLY ONE REALITY THAT KILLS

Book Four of The Sleeper Series
It happens to everyone without exception. It will inevitably happen to you unless you live under the wing of the legend.

LIE MAKES ME LIVE

Book Five of The Sleeper Series
This game of the intelligence, we were either to see through it, or die.
Coming soon

Also By Anna Schlegel
THE DEAD BANK DIARY SERIES

THE DEAD BANK DIARY
Book One of The Dead Bank Diary Series
The rats living on the refuse of the bank's backyard stay full at all time.

FOR THOSE IN THE SHADE
Book Two of The Dead Bank Diary Series
You may live your whole life without getting to know who you are, and sometimes this is for the better.

THE PRINTS ON THE SNOWS OF YESTERYEAR
Book Three of The Dead Bank Diary Series
The best one to rob the bank is the banker himself.

SOME DAY I'LL HIT A BANK
Book Four of The Dead Bank Diary Series
The bomb lives to its internal time.

THE FROZEN DEBT
Book Five of The Dead Bank Diary Series
When totally nude have a look, maybe you still have the shoulder loops.

CONTENTS

AUTHOR'S NOTE

What do the defectors really want? Why do these people betray their country and friends? Why are some of those defectors lucky, while some others are not? Why don't they ever have any regrets?

What are their true motives? Is it about money? No. Do they do it for fear? No. Do they sometimes wish to build their careers in this alternative way? No. Are they seeking fame? No. Have they been brainwashed? No. Can they be naive idealists? No.

Whatever answers you may think of, all of them would be probably wrong.

Are they betrayers? Yes, they are. Are they doing the right thing? Yes, they are. Do they find in this treachery what they must have been looking for? They sometimes do. How can they live with this? They are perfectly in tune with their own selves.

What are their goals? Now you will have the answer. It is worth knowing. This answer will surely change the way you see the world. This will be the answer from the legend.

The British intelligence cannot compromise its integrity, it will adhere to its principles like in the old times of rock 'n' roll. And it's damn good to look at it working... but then it's scary to see it work against you.

WHO SPREADS FOR WHOM

They seemed to be looking for a perfect witness for that legal action. One was a sleeper, another one a dead sleeper, and the third was a dummy agent. While this man alone passed for all three, but he was never summoned to court.

ABOUT THE SLEEPER SERIES

Each of the secret services has its own handwriting, faint and hardly perceptible. This handwriting is their custom, it does not change for years and one can read it through. This handwriting can lead the agent to failure. This is what these books are written about, if anything.

These books also tell of the legend that keeps recruiting people across time and distance, of something that is stronger than life. This legend is an eternal truth, refilled with the living blood of every new recruiter that would choose the way of the legend. These books are on the legend Kim Philby.

These books contain neither facts of Kim Philby's life nor any historical events. This is all about the modern-day and pure fiction.

I'm giving an answer to the question: Why the legend of Philby would be everlasting? Why is this legend of Philby of such a deadly pulling power? How do the people survive under the wing of his legend?

There is little said about it yet this is the main point.

They become traitors long before they step across the threshold of the spy directorate. They step across expressly to turn into traitors one fine day. That is the way they see their career. They wish to re-act that life of the icon. The legend of Kim Philby is making them traitors from the moment they open that book of his or read about him. This legend keeps recruiting people without money or contracts. The reality is forceless against it. The legend keeps dictating its own logic. It may come along imperceptibly, once the book of the legend is read through and half-forgotten, it would sprout up deep inside and live to its own time, so one day it would casually remind of its existence, in an implicit way, and push its follower to take the decision to which he must have been prepared since long, with just an occasion being in short supply.

Most paradoxically, such agents appear to be more mature, like everyone who does not really care much about public recognition, awards, money, appreciation and all those matters in connection with a regular rewarding career, they do not really fall for the uniform and regalia. Surely, the traitors gain incomparably better money, but it was not always this way, and would never be the main point. These people rate themselves so high that money does not measure that value. They are essentially free.

For such people there is no borderline where they become traitors, they must have since long slipped across by taking no notice. These people are usually well-educated and highbrow, and as much intelligently cruel and deeply calculating.

They are idealists. The philosophy of theirs makes blood turn to ice. This is how the legend of Kim Philby works. And that's a damn good British job.

CHAPTER ONE

DEATH OF THE SHADOW

Moscow-Berlin, February 2011

Two blocks from the house, Vlad and I separated and went in different directions. Vlad picked up a carton of mini cakes from me. When I glanced back his tracks were almost covered with dust snow, I turned and walked up to the hotel. I usually went up there towards evening and shortly went out again wearing makeup, as if going to spend the night in a bar.

In the lobby the receptionist came up to me and said in a soft voice,

"I'm so sorry, Frau Holt, your husband has died. Please accept my condolences."

What the hell was happening? I'd just parted from Vlad ten minutes earlier.

She nestled into my hand a slip of paper with the telephone number left by the police officer. It felt airless beyond endurance and I walked into the street and swallowed the chilly air. It must have taken some time to find me here. Just half an hour back ago I was buying my mini cakes. It could not be Vlad. *Oh Lord, let it be someone else, not Vlad!* But who?!

For another minute, frozen to the hotel porch in the scorching wind and the prickly glass-like powdery snow, I stared at the mirrored facade across the road. In the fine gauze of the casting joints it looked like freshly broken ice, and I was looking into my own reflection flitting among the passing cars, thinking that all these things must have happened to someone else, not to me. I was totally clueless, and everything around me instantly turned pointless and scary in this meaninglessness. No, it was no death; I would have sensed it otherwise. It could not be true. It must have been something else.

I took a shortcut through the courtyards, up to the block of the abandoned two-storeyed houses where Vlad was supposedly waiting for me. But was he still there, waiting for me?

Vlad had been a husband of mine for over a year now, per the documents, but we had actually made our first acquaintance right here, just about two weeks earlier. He was not Vlad Holt. The name Vlad Holt was only used for the deal's purposes, as that of the shadow partner. The name used to be passed from one shadow partner to another. Thus it had also become a name of mine, and I was supposed to gradually replace Vlad and become his back-up, Vlada Holt.

As to his daily life, Vlad lived under a different name, that of Andreas Leman, yet another assumed name. Over twenty years earlier he'd had been an American, Harvey Smith, a sleeper agent well forgotten by everyone since he'd moved to Berlin. In the course of the past two weeks we'd lost the bank that used to handle the deal transactions, they'd burnt up Vlad's identity – and these two weeks felt like a single night long trogglehumper. And then it had turned out to be not quite a nightmare, and everything Vlad had been talking about and all those things seemingly on his mind only had suddenly turned out to be a reality totally different from anything I had ever faced before, if I had ever faced it I might have passed through, taking no notice. Yet it was all properly there, and I could sometimes feel it in much – the way that with doors closed tight we can still sense the bustle of the street, the rustling of a hundred footsteps trampling through the melting snow, the voices, the road traffic noise and the smell of petrol.

In fact, I began to understand. Vlad was telling me he had made himself the identity documents a long time back during topsy-turvy times in these parts. His current passport was a true one; they used to make such passports for fugitives or undocumented aliens by pinning down a similar-looking person in the police archives – someone who had fled the country, and pasting in a different photo instead of the original one. There was a chance the man might come back and claim he'd lost his old passport, so they would issue another passport to him. In this way Vlad had procured his passport in the name of Vlad Holt. This possibility had existed until quite recently in some Eastern European countries, but at present, however, it was hardly feasible.

The real Vlad Holt had been a resident of New York for many years, and the chance he could have come up here in a coffin... *Oh Lord, was he really inside the coffin?!* ...were quite low.

If the real Vlad Holt had arrived in Berlin safe and sound, it would have hardly come to light. But he appeared to have turned up dead.

Holy shit, this is what must have really happened. And it had occurred at this particular point in time, today, when Vlad finally succeeded in getting rid of his Harvey Smith ghost for good.

After making my way around the block from the other side, I came back up to the café where we'd parted with Vlad. Fear made me cautious. I stopped opposite the shop window and surveyed the surrounding area in the glass reflection. There was no one to be seen. In my reflection I saw a pale, sharp face, my hair clotted with snow and my lips chapped with too bright a lipstick, my frozen gaze filled with fear. This reflection in the street lights was a clear picture, slightly vacillating and sliding that pulled me in as if I was looking at my other self inside the café somewhere in between those tables, myself in some other life. Behind my back the light snow dusted the dark garden across the street from the gray skies that looked whiter and whiter in the light of the street lamps, and soon there was nothing to be seen beyond the snow.

I walked along, looking under my feet into the gray footstep medley in the melting snow at both edges of the walkway exposed in the middle. Vlad's footprints were barely visible, a trace more snow and they would totally disappear. Indeed, I could see his footprints in the yard and at the porch by the door. In the frigid air of the stair well I could smell his cigarette smoke. Every step of mine champing against the brick rubble echoed in the void inside of the old building.

This apartment of ours in an abandoned house in the suburbs was pledged by the bank and was intended to serve as a shelter for a few days, but we had been staying there for two weeks already. How much longer were we supposed to live there? I had better not think about it.

I pushed the door into the anteroom.

"Vlad!"

For a split second I seemed to be calling into vacancy. Then a chair squeaked aside in the kitchen. Oh my goodness, he was at home!

"Vlad! What does that mean, your badass mother?!"

Vlad had no idea. For another minute he stood there, frozen to the spot in bewilderment, in the middle of the room. All we knew for sure was that Vlad was alive; to hell with everything else. Vlad had seemed exhausted for the past few days.

"Vodka?" I offered.

"Yes. With cranberry. I'd rather not think of anything now. Damn it all."

Worst of all, everything that had befallen Vlad actually had nothing to do with him, so there was very little he could do. Obviously, Vlad was supposed to play a witness in court, a proper convenient and dead witness, as sleeper agent Harvey Smith. It would not be so easy to turn him into a live witness.

The small bank of Schumann was in charge of transactions for a Russian company trading in military equipment. This company held some other accounts on this side, in several major banks like Kommerzbank, Deutsche Bank and Dresdner Bank, all these banks connected to the case of money laundering in relation to BoNY. None of these banks seemed to be involved in any other illegal operations and would not have lodged any transactions for these accounts. Presumably, in their effort to overblow the scandal the Americans must have intended to make Schumann disclose this transaction history. For that matter they would have been required to put some pressure on Schumann. Why not? Initially we had found it hard to understand why, apart from money laundering, they could accuse Schumann of espionage for the benefit of the Russians. It looked absurd, but that was only in case they had no evidence. However, to all appearances, there must have been some evidence.

It looked as if Schumann's defense had found an ideal witness in Harvey Smith, a sleeper who used to work alongside Schumann for an audit company in San Francisco, a man who had been well forgotten by everyone for over twenty years. On his side Schumann would have also looked a similar long-discarded agent.

How could they have learned of Harvey Smith? Vlad could only guess.

It was clear the British Intelligence had been giving away and covering the banker Schumann at the same time. This seemed utterly absurd. However Vlad had been looking at it from a different angle, and he had a reason. He'd thought the British Intelligence must have been constrained to give the banker away with their source still duly concealed. At the same time, if the British had been under pressure to disclose their source, then instead of the man they would have presented the dead body of Andreas Leman. And their London source due to some god damn circumstances had been the banker Schumann himself. And so the man had found a witness for himself. In the course of these two weeks we could sense them doing their best to cover the source by all means possible.

Initially, there had been given a tip-off. Somewhere in the archive records or in someone's memory there must have flashed information that Harvey Smith resided in Berlin under the name of Andreas Leman. Where could this lead have come from? Could it have been in his case file? We could only speculate.

Today Andreas Leman was just in time to draw his confession and reconfirm he used to be an agent under the name of Harvey Smith. This statement was extinguished by his lawyer right away. Who would ever need any confession written for money? The ex-agent Harvey Smith appeared no longer good for this court, with or without evidence, neither alive nor dead, under the name of Andreas Leman, so Vlad had the chance to survive. And after making his way home as usual, through several quarters aslant the courtyards, with a stop at the café, where I'd bumped into him at the doorstep, to assure me he was free as a bird, he'd taken a carton of mini-cakes from my hands and continued on his way home, and I'd left for the hotel.

I had no wish to think on. Vlad had survived, and he seemed not to believe it himself the fact he was still alive... How many times over these past days had he been asking himself that question and wondering why he might be still alive?

Then something must have happened and the sleeper agent Harvey Smith had turned up again in these parts under the name of Vlad Holt. Was he really there? *Oh my god, was he there inside the coffin?!...* The man had turned up dead way too fast, in the blink of an eye.

Obviously, Vlad Holt, the true German under whose passport Vlad had been living all this time, and whom Vlad resembled somewhat, could not have died so suddenly. Well, his body must have been sent over here so that he could play a witness in Berlin. They'd truly wanted a convenient dead witness.

And along with this man Vlad had also expired. Vlad appeared a shadow of the real Vlad Holt, and now, just like in a fairy tale, the master was dead and his shadow died along with him, however real it might have been. At first,

Vlad had been burned up as agent Harvey Smith, and now he appeared to have been totally scratched off. He existed no more. Was he still there as Andreas Leman? Hardly so. Andreas Leman was tightly bound to Harvey Smith.

Vlad told me to go to his apartment and take care of the obsequies. There were two people and two different lawyers. Andreas Leman had a lawyer who'd successfully snatched the sleeper away from the case just before the court. Vlad Holt had his own lawyer so I could go and meet him. Would he remember Vlad?

"Vlad, my name is Vlada Holt..."

"So what? A beautiful Estonian woman and a quick romance at the seacoast ... It was fate, why not?"

"There is no way this could be a coincidence."

"Uh-huh, you could bury me and enjoy life. They have already found you. Do you remember? You've been just contacted by the police in the hotel. If you don't turn up for the funeral of your own husband it will look odd. So what's the telephone number?" Vlad took from my hands the slip with the number left by the policeman. "Make a call and let them help you with the paperwork."

I dialed the number and presented myself.

"Ernest Hoffmann. I work for a private security agency," he replied as he had been expecting my call. "You could walk up your apartment and then see the lawyer," he gave me the lawyer's name.

"Private security agency. What could it be? Who is this man?" I asked Vlad.

Vlad suggested this Hoffmann might be the link we had to the counterintelligence, the case of the banker Schumann could not have been lost on them. Anyway, there was no one else but him.

In the morning, when I opened the door to his small apartment atop a modest downtown building, where Vlad used to live under the name of Vlad Holt, I caught sight of a parcel on the table. It was a regular postal package. Inside there was a cinerary urn of Vlad Holt, his death certificate and some documents from the lawyer's office that had forwarded the urn. The man had died a week earlier. I looked round. The apartment was rather small, it held nothing extra and a fresh bed sheet smell, yet it did not seem uninhabited, but as if its owner had just left. Through the half-open door to the kitchen I could see some cups and an ashtray on the table, and the kitchen sink was filled with plates, two empty whiskey bottles were standing on the floor. If I had not known Vlad, it would seem a common bachelor's house. Vlad, the way I saw him, would never have left any dirty plates, he had no habit of doing so. It crossed my mind, *A guy may relax and rest from his own self here.* Or then maybe, he was usually here the way I had never seen him, unshaven, stoop-shouldered and plain, with a fastidious glance hardly noticeable behind the dim reflection of his round glasses, which made him look almost blind?

Vlad had informed me a neighbor of his had the keys, as he used to leave quite often, so she must have opened the door for the postman. Or could someone else have visited the place already?

The lawyer's office was close by, in an old house with the name plates of several attorneys listed at the entrance. Attorney Yakov Rivkin was an elderly man with a soft wrinkled face as if flowing down a forehead that looked pulled on his skull mapping beneath his bald pate, with his neck tendons strained under his silk tie. He was not surprised. He'd called the lawyer in New York and the latter had confirmed Vlad Holt's desire to be buried here in his homeland.

"He was not divorced. Were you been aware of that?" Rivkin inquired.

I knew that. Vlad had once told me about his research on the real Vlad Holt; the man had a wife and three children.

The attorney asked me how long I had been in Berlin. I replied that as per Vlad, he'd been willing to live together after the partition of their property, but then somehow it'd all lingered. Our marriage had been solemnized a year ago, in Tallinn. Well, of course I'd had no idea that his family was in America ... Just a week earlier Vlad had told me it was all done with, and that I was to get ready to travel to Berlin, while waiting for his call. I'd hopped to it and arrived here a week early, to stay in a hotel. I'd just wanted to take a tour of Berlin by night, to have an idea of where I was going to live now, and actually sell myself on the idea of it being true. I replied I had not known of him not being divorced, and of him living in the States.

"I don't think his family will wish to come for his funeral, after they learn he used to have another family on this side," I said.

"A romance on the seacoast? That may happen to a man over forty," the attorney replied in the same way as Vlad had told me this earlier.

Rivkin told me if that Holt's wife ever came, or some other relatives of his arrived from New York, he would let me know.

I guessed the lawyer was somewhat suspicious, but I was unable to read anything on his face. Vlad Holt appeared to be a real person, with his residential rental bills and credit cards... Oh, might this lawyer have made a call to someone up on my departure? I had no idea. The American Vlad Holt must have been holding his German passport, the one he used to live with in this country. It should have been illegal, but there was no one to blame any more. Or could have Hoffman settled it for us?

Vlad Holt was dead and Vlad would have to expire along with him, there was no choice. There should have been just a single Vlad Holt.

The lawyer promptly made the arrangements so in a couple of hours with the urn in my hands I was in a taxi on my way to Zehlendorf Cemetery. Looking through the window at the gray city under the falling snow I dwelled on something else. How could that other wife of Vlad Holt have learned that her husband had another wife? They must have been living a common life, the man would come home from his office daily and generally have no secrets either from his wife or from friends, everything must have been transparent. And then suddenly it had turned out to be a soap opera. It was about treachery. How would I have felt in her shoes? No way. I had never been in her shoes as I'd never really wanted it. I had Ilya, but things were so much different with him.

One day Vlad had asked me,

"Doesn't your husband tell you lies?"

Every single minute, I'd almost said offhandedly. Then after giving it some thought, I'd replied,

"Every single minute."

And that's why I felt so easy with Ilya. Ilya valued me and he did not want to lose me, this was the main thing. And the rest was nothing.

Soon I was standing at the cemetery wall where I placed the funeral urn. It was colder in these parts than downtown. The surroundings looked somewhat brighter and edgy, the way you see things in an old black and white photograph, just the snow with some black trunks of pine trees under the snowcaps, and the gray tombstones in between the pathways full of snow. For a split second I felt uneasy, thinking this could have been Vlad. What if I were to bury him at this point? My toes were numb in my sodden boots, and all I wanted was get back soon and put those boots on the radiator to dry, then have a cup of hot coffee. Vlad was right, he'd come out alive, and the hell with everything else. But how come he was alive? Something must have happened.

From afar I could see an elderly gentleman approaching me in a dark coat with a white doughy somewhat melted face under the black hat, with his eyes, too black and sunken deep into his face, like charcoal heated by the sun and fallen into a melting snowball. He gave me a nod when he came up, said *Hoffmann,* and took me by the arm. Who was he? Hell if I knew.

I still had some polite questions spinning in my mind, such as *Have you been familiar with my husband?* and other such nonsense. But then, after screening his face, I realized this question was more than necessary, and that he actually knew enough. Hoffmann was staying silent, and slowly we started for the exit.

When telling me goodbye he invited me to drop in at his place for a cup of tea any time. This would not bind me to anything really.

On my way back from the cemetery I walked up to the hotel past the sympathetic eyes of the receptionist, and took off my boots to dry, then I got warm under the hot shower, opened my laptop and entered the name: Vlad Holt, New York, date of birth 1960, place of birth Berlin. There was no text about his death, nothing at all, nothing personal. I found his family, his wife and children. They had everything the usual way, their posts and selfies with friends, all those things so easy to find on the internet. It looked as if Vlad Holt had never existed.

What the hell was happening?

CHAPTER TWO

DAMN GOOD-LOOKING

Vlad was to hand over to me all participants to the deal and then withdraw from the business. I was stand in for Vlad.

There were over a hundred partners and middlemen, including functionaries, military establishment members, diplomats and company leads. For some of them it was enough to give a warning by phone the deal was tied up for the time being, but others were so mistrustful and cautious that whole thing was out of the question for them if Vlad wasn't there.

Vlad always remained in the shadows. Not so many partners had ever seen his face. However they knew Vlad was there and they could reach him on call in case something went wrong, but the deal went on like clock work so they rarely met Vlad in person. He was known as Vlad Holt only to the middlemen involved in this deal.

It was rather hard to discover Vlad Holt, and even harder to figure out that the shadow partner to the deal named Vlad Holt and a sleeper agent of whom no one had recollected in the last twenty years, a US citizen Harvey Smith, were one and the same person.

But somehow they managed to find out.

The invader probably knew Vlad was the clue to the whole scheme. It meant the invader had the secret services at his command. But then it should have been the Russians, not the British, damn it all!

Two days earlier Vlad had managed to warn everyone he knew.

Some of the partners had wished to meet Vlad in person right away; others had agreed to see him later. In the beginning I'd found it hard to understand the whole setup and kept asking myself, *Why would all of them wish to see him in person? Could they read things from his face or something?*

It had turned out to be so. They had been truly reading Vlad's face when passing by in the park, in a single hurried glance. One of the partners, a tall and wizened man with sunken cheeks and a vulture-like crooked nose, had stopped, and by taking a greedy pull on his vape, had glimpsed Vlad, then with a bit of curiosity me, from under the palm covering his face. This had been enough for him. He had given us a slight nod and quickened his pace. Vlad had only taken me along to his appointments with the major partners. Until that encounter I had been unaware of the fact Vlad was so valued and realized I would never be able to replace him. I would never become for them the kind of person Vlad used to be.

Vlad was like a love-mate to some of them, one could tell this by the way they looked at him; it could not be interpreted otherwise. And they had a reason. Vlad was a sex bomb, something like a male edition of Marilyn Monroe, aged fifty, a stretched vest on his broad crooked shoulders, unshaven, in his well worn jeans.

He was a bright-looking blonde with delicate, flushed and weather-bitten skin in hardly-noticeable freckles. His sun-bleached eyebrows and bloodless lips seemed to vanish in his face. His glance was hard, condescending and cold, as if his eyes had iced up under those hoarfrost-like eyelashes. Initially I'd been avoiding any eye contact with him as he seemed looking right through me, as if I was not there. And when Vlad asked me questions, he was pulling every answer from me along with my intestines with that glance of his.

Whatever Vlad had been telling me, he was a true agent, and his main feature was this knowledge of how to tempt people in, whatever job he was doing. Vlad could easily tempt both men and women. His charm was a killing power and he knew to take advantage of it. It was not of pure awareness but this skill was rather well-trained so one could feel it, like a touch of satisfaction gloss on a respectable businessman or by a BMW standing at the porch, of which you start thinking once you see the man. Darn good-looking. I was not used to that kind of man.

"Do you fancy me?" Vlad had put this question indifferently, hardly looking at me from under his spectacles, catching my eye which I'd failed to hide in time.

"Yeah, badass mother, you're just like a Russian icon, beautiful sad and gloomy."

"Who's about to seize the deal? I also do appreciate your behind. And the British Intelligence... It's enough to drive me mad," Vlad had muttered.

Vlad found it not so easy to reconcile to my dubbing him. At first he hardly spoke to me, it seemed I was a misunderstanding to him. However, the payments for that deal had to be transferred to some Moscow bank the sooner the better, so after all it seemed rather convenient. If the whole arrangement was restored the settlements would be processed via Moscow, Vlad and I would part company to keep the deal under control on two sides, I would do it in Moscow and he would work in Berlin.

Would I be happy to play Vlada Holt? I had not given it a minute's thought, I truly wanted to stay in that deal in whatever way or function it could be, to feel it all in my hands... Damn, something there always went wrong, and I was in for it along with the person who was officially my husband.

I wished at least something of that deal could persist in the long run... But would there remain anything at all? At this point my hope seemed rather silly. So what about Vlad? Would he still be there?

While being toffee nosed Vlad was rather undemanding. He kept endlessly washing his underwear, and when in the kitchen he would set to cleaning and cooking something. His hands motion and gestures seemed quite habitual and skillful, so I thought he probably had a sick mother or a little child. He'd never told me of having a family and I had no idea what his life might have been here in Berlin, most likely he did have a family. How could he have left them? He'd left without telling anyone, as per his own words.

"Vlad, you don't have to cook, you've got a woman for that," I said dropping into the kitchen.

"It's not for you, mein herz. Back off. You know nothing about it," Vlad said this the way he might as well say it was snowing, as if he'd already learnt everything about me.

Looking at Vlad I thought that if he'd spread for some wealthy businessman, someone involved in the deal, he could have been enjoying life on board his own yacht or in a golf club somewhere.

Vlad easily guessed what I was thinking.

"I can't do it that way. I should make money on my own. I've got some project of life. And it's all linked to you, mein herz. I am not able to raid the banks the way you do."

If only I could! I used to work as a stock market trader, and after losing my job I'd lived on some random transactions or simply on doles picking occasions to raid some minor bank on the verge of bankruptcy. Many people were involved with illegal takeovers, and it seemed not so very complicated, the banks used to fall into hands just like fish from a full sea, but I was a total failure. Yet we still required a modest little bank through which we could process payments for this deal.

"I have tried to do it several times before but failed, Vlad."

"We do need a bank. Just think about it. We got to preserve this scheme. Can't you see ... the beauty of it?" Vlad found it hard to find a proper word, the deal was so dear to him.

"...like those parables of Zoroaster?" I guessed.

"Hmm, you are quite receptive," Vlad froze for a moment from my being able to read his mind, "So get the hell off."

I left the hotel late in the evening. The trees in the petty fairy lights looked like foam that had drifted ashore along the bed of the highway that carried multiple car lights. And right there, behind the residential buildings, everything disappeared, and those courtyards of ours remained dark and empty, and I could feel this void from afar. There was not a single illuminated window to be seen in the evenings. Here and there the reflections of passing car lights along the dark windows. We also lived here invisibly, but had it been the kind of invisibility we wanted to believe in?

Waiting for death here... How could Vlad keep thinking of it? How could he remain expectant? How had he managed to survive over these last few days? They had been cold, transparent and high-sounding, the kind of sound made by a cup falling from your hands against the parquet, were its clinking upon break-up would resonate as a shiver through your whole body.

Vlad had entered this apartment two weeks earlier as a different man. Or had it only seemed so to me? At present he looked rather faded and drawn, the wrinkles around his lips had sharpened, he was unshaven and his overgrown bristle made him look old and frigid. I had been with him all this time, but I found it unbearable to look at him now. He was walking noiselessly as a shadow. What were his chances of staying in hiding here? Of course, there was none, it was just a mere grace. Initially I had not been able to see the reason why Vlad was just waiting it out. He seemed free to go any place and escape, by making himself some other identity papers. Ultimately, he had some professional contacts that could assist in his disappearance without a trace.

Vlad had once told me, *Not of the British Intelligence, mein herz.*

He'd never wanted anyone else to get a view of the secret services due to him.

That time I'd inquired,

"Vlad, the British Intelligence, is it really what I guess it to be?"

As per Vlad, it might have been not the secret service as such, but some kind of a retired agent working for a major security agency. It did happen; the old men could leave their jobs, by leading away the people they used to work with. Someone might have hired the man. But really, they'd been too expedient in delivering of the urn... Judging by the fact that the British had been under pressure to give away the banker Schumann to the Americans, it must have been the work of the Intelligence, and not a retired agent with whatever good connections he might have.

"The hand is too obvious," Vlad had told me. "A single agent working more or less independently would not have left such a trace."

Vlad had told me, the more important the operation the agent was assigned to, the better one could see its handwriting; all and all major operations were subject to continuous agreement, review and adjustment by the management, and the agent was never free-handed to make any decision, everything was supposed to be dictated to him.

"Vlad, do you think this operation with the banker Schumann is a major one?"

"Schumann is the side we can observe, which is tangible to me."

When Vlad brought up the British Intelligence, I had a feeling he was checking out all those things that had happened to him against a set of invisible guidelines, which were prescribed and followed by every person involved with the British Service, whether the man wanted it or not. They appeared to carry this logic along like the painters unable to shake off the skills developed in their old school eventually fail to create a painting of their own. Every school would leave its trace on the picture, especially obvious with the young people. The best school is the one of which its graduates can, after completing their course, forget once and for all and take their own way, free of its load. But in fact, very few people appear capable of dropping the load.

No, the British or any other secret service is not about offices packed with high-tech electronics worth a moderate state budget, nor about databases nor any other assets. All this had never really helped to find anyone. The camera might trace a person yet it cannot really open up any archives reserved for staff only. And once a traitor turned up, it could be only due to another traitor having spoken about him, a defector Joe, or another recruited agent. The source of information could be these people only. Against any traitor there was always another traitor. And the whole setup remained this way, the same as a hundred years back, just like sex, there are a lot of new toys coming out every year but the essence remains unchanged.

Strangely, I could not find anything on Vlad Holt, I was curious to see whether Vlad truly resembled his passport duplicate.

"Vlad, I've found nothing on Vlad Holt, no obituary notice, and nothing at all about him, not even a single photo of his. It's as if he never existed," I told him right from the doorstep, taking off my coat and brushing snow from the hood.

"Really? Has someone cleaned out everything? I used to find some records of him earlier. The man used to work for a consulting company. There is something fishy underway," Vlad wanted to say something else but I interrupted him,

"Vlad, at this point the family of Vlad Holt must have learned about him being remarried. It's cruel and weird, and I feel bad about it, Vlad."

"Could we do without hysterics?" Vlad cut me short. "We don't know anything about his family. Families differ. You should not think too much. When the time comes you'll give a call to his wife and tell her this has been a mistake. You'll tell her that... Well, you'd better guard words. If that marriage was a genuine story, his wife would rather believe you."

"Could he have really wished to be buried in Berlin? Far from his family? Can you believe it? Vlad we're engaged in a weird battle. Vlad Holt couldn't have died at such a good hour. They murder..."

"Oh God, what is on your mind?! No, they don't really kill anyone. We just can't see things right off the way they are in reality... I don't know how to explain it. Remember that tail after me? It was the kind of surveillance I've been used since a young age. It was the kind I was supposed to notice. Try to look at it through my eyes. We've got to double check everything. So much might be nothing but a mere illusion of yours, so until you probe the bullet in my corpse, you shouldn't believe in my murder. Until you see my dead body in the mortuary, you shouldn't believe I'm dead. Have a look, I've got a scar under my chin," Vlad threw back his chin so I could see his scar, it was hardly visible. "That is why I don't like shaving... So make sure it's truly me, don't you believe in everything. You'll understand what I mean, over time. You'll get used to thinking the way I do. Could you make it faster? Otherwise you won't be able to survive. This is not the criminal world, they don't really solve their issues by killing people, and they are the Intelligence. Intelligence people only do the needful. Is that clear now?" Vlad fixed his deadpan eyes on my face to make sure I got it, and then he grew sulky and added, "Fuck, something is telling me they would go out of their way to do all the needful for me. And we've got nothing but the naked ass."

"Vlad, all I can see is murder. I will never be able to see things the way you see them," I responded stubbornly, by taking my boots off and setting them on the kitchen radiator.

Earlier Vlad had figured out their intention to draw a confession out of him, that he used to be Harvey Smith, a Lubyanka agent recruited some twenty years back.

However, it appeared a lot more convenient to just get him killed and throw in some evidence, then have a death letter written in his name with a proper confession statement. Usually, the easiest way to go was the most reasonable one. Vlad could sense things might turn out that way. It appeared too much obvious. What else was I supposed to think after I had just left the funeral urn of Vlad Holt at the cemetery, happy to get its weight off my hands?

Vlad had chosen not to wait. He had drawn up a statement and then turned into common businessman Andreas Leman. Thus he had survived.

Was it far too easy? True, since no one would have been able to link him to Harvey Smith. The confession of Andreas Leman might have been the only link. There had remained nothing of Harvey Smith, no trace, everything had been properly cleaned up after his departure, yet it all looked as though he had disappeared. Harvey Smith had left San Francisco for Johannesburg twenty years ago. He'd left as if he'd intended to come back later, without closing out his accounts. He had neither sold his apartment nor his car, and he had never mentioned to anyone his intention not to come back. He'd gone missing.

Vlad was sure there was a case file of Harvey Smith that along with his twenty-year-old photo was in the name of Andreas Leman. To what extent could resemblance count? Was it really so easy to recognize a person twenty years after? Their resemblance and the coincidence of the surnames would not really count as evidence. Andreas Leman would not have left the US embassy so easily, if they had had at least something to prove that he'd been Harvey Smith, something more solid than just his own words and this likeness.

That time we hadn't known there was another bigger reason for Andreas Leman to walk out the embassy door so easily.

They hardly could have predicted the ability of Andreas Leman to move forward with that confession statement of his. That is why, when Vlad told me they would kill him, I truly believed it. It seemed so simple and clear. When protecting your own life by aiming your gun at someone, they say, it's always better to shoot in the head so that the attacker would never be able to tell anything in court, lest he turns up in a wheelchair. The jury would only consider one version of events, it would be yours. True, the dead body of Andreas Leman with that confession of him being Harvey Smith would have been the only version. However, you never know what to expect from someone alive. A flesh and blood person could change his story any time, while a dead man never will.

The stiff Andreas Leman as sleeper agent Harvey Smith was supposed to reconfirm in court that the banker Martin Schumann had been a similar harmless sleeper. There seemed no other explanation as to why they would require a long-forgotten sleeper like him, in fact, we could see none.

"Vlad, what the hell this Hoffmann is inviting me for a cup of tea? What does he mean? Who is he? Is he a retired counterspy?"

"If Hoffmann is aware of what is going on and of the deal itself, he must think we are seeking to get rid of the partners now, and some of them might fall into his hands. He is just eager to make some money."

"Is it so evident what exactly we are going to do?"

"These are the game rules... Wait," Vlad instantly froze to the spot with a guess, moved his glasses up his forehead, all adrift, and then rubbed his face with his palm, "I just thought... has everything really been cleaned up? Oh, shit! What if that Vlad Holt has been playing the former me, Harvey Smith? Damn it... Well, and the ashes of that American Vlad Holt have been sent over here as the ashes of Harvey Smith. This is clear. Otherwise why would they have delivered it straight away by the court date? Sure, he looks like a stone-dead source. But what if he'd been Harvey Smith for a while?"

"What?!"

It flashed through my mind, *How can Vlad keep thinking that way? What has he really got on his mind? And how much time will it take before I start thinking the way he does? A hundred or a thousand years?*

"Those bastards, they give us no rest, not a single minute," Vlad cussed and poured himself a pownie of cranberry vodka, then seemed to forget about it, and started smoking absentmindedly, then finally uttered, "He could have been Harvey Smith without knowing it... he could have become me, Harvey Smith, at any point..."

"Vlad... that is a bit too much, that sounds like delirium," I said, and then something came to my mind. "Vlad, can they really play the card of Harvey Smith twice in the same court process? It has already been played. Andreas Leman paid them a visit and signed his confession of being ex-agent Harvey Smith. And so what? Now they'll get these ashes of the

American Vlad Holt as the ashes of Harvey Smith? Isn't that too much for a court process?"

"No, but can't you see the card is getting played over again right in your hands now? You've been holding it today."

I shrugged, either from the draft touching across my blades coming from the vent sash, or of those words of his. Supposing this guess of his was correct, which meant that Harvey Smith had not been a sleeper and had not disappeared but had continued his work as an agent. If that was the case, Harvey Smith had not been a harmless sleeper, but an operative. If that consulting firm manager Vlad Holt had been this agent Harvey Smith, things really did look different, didn't they?

From Vlad's wink I understood he had almost no doubt.

And what might this Vlad Holt have been doing as an agent? Who could have killed him and put his ashes into that urn, then sent it to Berlin at such a good hour? Could this have been no murder? However much I was trying to push that thought aside, there was no retreat. The concept was so simple and clear, I could read it through so easily. Why couldn't it have been the reality?

CHAPTER THREE

BURNED CARD

Thus, the ashes of Vlad Holt had been sent over here as the ashes of the agent Smith. How could one believe this, the agent Smith had just been businessman Andreas Leman? The whole story had changed overnight, the day when Andreas Leman had put that confession of his in black and white.

There was an answer. Indeed, we'd been thinking there must have been a case file of Smith with a photo of his, dated twenty years back, and a record that read he was living in Berlin under the name of Andreas Leman. And this photograph might have been seen by US Embassy translator Michael Brown. Who would have ever thought Vlad's life could be in the hands of one Michael Brown, a plump middle-aged man with a tired crumpled face, a smooth bold head and a mountain of debts? Michael Brown worked as the embassy translator and he was one of the middlemen in the deal. Could any of the middlemen have known that shadow partner Vlad Holt was living in Berlin as a common businessman under the name of Andreas Leman? Someone might have known. But for sure no one could have known this Leman used to be Harvey Smith. Vlad had most forgotten this himself. One could have only learned about it when looking at the photo of Smith in his case file.

We were thinking the case file had resurfaced at the Embassy. In what other way could we explain the agent Smith turned out to be not Andreas Leman but Vlad Holt?

Most importantly, by taking a look at that old photo Brown must have recognized the man not as Andreas Leman, whom he had never met, but Vlad Holt, the person in charge of the deal that involved the buyup of several African countries' foreign debts. He had recognized the agent in that man, as the supervision of a deal of that scale was a job for a special agent.

That is why there must have been a case file or some other records. Otherwise, how could this Michael Brown have learned as much? Beside him, there seemed to be no one else able to recognize Vlad Holt in Harvey Smith.

Initially we'd been thinking there was no one but Michael Brown who was able to identify him in the photo. But later on Vlad admitted that they must have long known of him as Vlad Holt. The situation with Michael Brown seemed a bit complicated. He was obviously a Russian informant in the Embassy. By looking at him Vlad could see the man was underpaid. Most probably, after having noticed the photo of Smith dated twenty years ealier, Brown had reported to Moscow, but he'd somehow told it to the wrong person, and thus he must have hastened events. However, at this point it did not matter.

The long and the short of it, upon his appointment with Vlad, Michael Brown had made the decision to strike colors. Whether he had yielded himself on his own accord, or whether they had been informed of him already, was not the point. Vlad had put his mind to burning him up, yet he had not done so. Michael might have guessed that Vlad, if he'd been working for Moscow, was aware of him, so those others must have learned things as well.

What could Michael Brown have revealed at the interrogation? Each and every thing he knew. The man was aware that it was a major deal, and he knew the surnames of several partners. He also knew that the payments within this arrangement had been underway for quite a number of years, and the whole thing was controlled by a shadow partner, by German named Vlad Holt who resembled the old photo of former agent Harvey Smith, the man who'd changed his name upon his arrival to Berlin for Andreas Leman. But the same might have changed his name yet another time, to become Vlad Holt. He could have wanted to cut the strings of Moscow, right? It actually made no difference.

In fact, there was no reason to doubt the information Michael Brown must have leaked. With all that, Harvey Smith must have turned into this German Vlad Holt, and under the same name must have returned to New York. If someone had ever wanted to see the identity documents against which the man had been issued a German passport in the name of Vlad Holt twenty years back, then opposite the name of Vlad Holt they would have found the photo of... Andreas Leman. Or what? They must have also hacked the records, and the photo of Holt must taken back into the fold.

Andreas Leman was still alive and had just paid a visit to the Embassy. This Harvey Smith had probably lived with the Leman's passport for a short while only, then instantly changed it for the passport of Vlad Holt which used the same photo of Andreas Leman. There was a clear resemblance between him and Harvey Smith. The man must have left for New York to become American citizen Vlad Holt.

If they had discovered any photos of the American Holt, it would have been clear Andreas Leman resembled the young Harvey Smith more than Harvey Smith himself, the one who had become the American Holt. However Andreas Leman was nothing but a businessman. And this Andreas Leman appeared was of no interest to anyone. That meant there could be a Vlad Holt, a plain German citizen, who didn't know about any other person living in New York under his name.

In fact, one could pick up these two Germans, Andreas Leman and also track down Vlad Holt. But they were both mere victims of identity theft. There was no chance of making them into special agents in court.

The agent Harvey Smith living in New York under the name of Vlad Holt seemed a more interesting target.

As per Vlad, if that American Vlad Holt had everything properly cleaned up, there were probably no recent photos of him. And if anyone thought of searching Vlad Holt's apartment at his residence address in Berlin they would have found the fingerprints of the American Vlad Holt? That didn't seemed so difficult to arrange.

The most deadly point was that, this Michael Brown could have seen Andreas Leman enter the US Embassy. If he had seen Leman, the game was over. Otherwise, if Michael Brown had not really seen Leman with his own eyes, we might still have a chance. In effect, Michael Brown appeared to be the only dangerous link. He would be able to destroy this new legend of agent Harvey Smith, deceased under the name of Vlad Holt a week earlier in New York.

And then, could someone else have taken care of Brown so that he would not see Leman, and would not be able to identify the shadow partner Vlad Holt in him, like the Kray Twins?

No one else from the embassy had seen Vlad Holt alive; Michael Brown was the last see him.

In Vlad's thoughts, the moment Andreas Leman had entered the US Embassy, they must have already been informed that American Vlad Holt had been dead for a week or so, and his ashes must have been already on the way to Berlin. While translator Michael Brown could have been at that particular time on a flight to Washington for further interrogation and jail. Surely, he could have been shown a video record of Andreas Leman entering the US Embassy. Otherwise, some time later he'd have seen Leman anyway.

Michael Brown had suddenly evolved into the most critical witness. Of course, it could have been easy to find the photo of Vlad Holt in the archives. But only the man to identify in that very photo the shadow partner Vlad Holt and not Andreas Leman, could have been no one else but Michael Brown. Anyone else would have identified Andreas Leman. And what did that German citizen Holt look like? Surely, they could eventually find some pictures of the American Vlad Holt show to Michael Brown. And if he saw them, he would tell them that the man in the picture was a different person.

And the defunct Michael Brown had no chance of ever seeing any of this.

Michael Brown could have had another heart attack at the interrogation, or else... Vlad had met Michael Brown in a café at the railway station a few days back. That was the place where Michael Brown had suffered his heart attack. We had not seen it happen, I had only noticed Michael Brown make a few steps away from the table he'd taken to talk to Vlad, and his faltering gait, and then, a small crowd had gathered, and I'd seen some medical personnel spring up. That was it. So Michael Brown could be doing his time in hospital, or he could have died already. This seemed to be the only valid explanation for the fact that no one was interested in Andreas Leman any more

Andreas Leman, when entering the Embassy, looked like another person who wished to partake of the suspects list for hijacker D.B. Cooper. There seemed to be no valid evidence of Andreas Leman being the agent Harvey Smith. All in all, in the suspects list for D.B. Cooper the first lines were filled with hijackers, and then the people who had the looks of those. And what could Andreas Leman have done to get onto the suspects list for agent Harvey Smith? Nothing. Well, a resemblance could sometimes cost you your life. How often do people lose their life due to some passing similarity? It would be better not to think about it.

Andreas Leman looked rather like a frame-up. That is why he had managed to escape so easily.

All things considered the banker Schumann awaiting espionage charges would hardly sit back and do nothing. It was quite and within reason to suggest he had been making up the list of potential witnesses against him, and Harvey Smith must have been on that list. He could not have forgotten his co-worker, could he? To ruin the case it was enough to palm off a wrong witness, someone like Andreas Leman. The man would have been rather easy to find, and then he would surely want the money.

The main thing was that all the translator Michael Brown could have revealed involved no deep knowledge of the long-forgotten agent. Vlad was still in control of the deal, doing the agent's job. And this was the most recent information, more truthful than any other evidence as Vlad Holt had appeared to be still alive, until quite recently, a bit more than a week ago, when they'd sent his ashes to Berlin.

Unable to understand things properly, I asked him,
"If Michael Brown is dead just because he could have identified in Andreas Leman the shadow partner Vlad Holt, and then inevitably linked Harvey Smith with

those two, does that mean they'd known about you? I mean the British? Who send the ashes of Holt over here? Apparently, this must have been done by the British. That is, they should have known since long of you being the real Harvey Smith that had later turned into the German Vlad Holt. How long could they have known this?"

"Surely they knew it. Do you think it's so easy to make a spy out of a common American, Holt?" Vlad said this as a matter-of-course but I could see he was still trying on this idea for size. "But they must have been equally aware that I'd turned into a plain businessman Leman. Well, I'd once again changed my name for Holt, which is quite natural. And have the British been as well informed of the deal's being under my supervision? I doubt that. In that case, everything Michael Brown might have told them was much like the Revelation of God."

"Then why haven't they found you as Vlad Holt, to bring you in as Smith? Why would they have needed the American Holt? Why is he any better than you? For some reason, they'd wanted this Leman. Could this have been due to that line in the case file? And how have they found Holt? I'm not understanding anything."

"It's somewhat more complicated," Vlad said in contemplatively, scratching the bristle on his chin. "No one knew I was the person in charge of the deal. They must have learned it just a few days ago from Michael Brown. And they must have been making the agent from that Holt guy for quite a while, so he must have eventually turned out better than the original. I guess many years back someone had afforded my protection by putting them on to that American Holt, so the man had come into view of FBI. The British only had to maintain that version for a while, a few years ago. The British actually had two options, either Leman or the American Holt. I think they've done a great job with that Holt, so that he could act as a witness in court against Schumann. I guess they would have grabbed a hold of that case file anyway. The British did not right away give out the ashes of Holt as those of Smith; they must have wanted to wait out until Leman is left alone. They could have helped me out with that lawyer, couldn't they? The British must have intended in some way to replace Leman for Holt, but how? I have no idea. However at that particular moment the idea to turn him in must have come to Michael Brown's mind. So Michael Brown, without his being aware of it, sort of redressed this situation by saying that Smith had become Holt."

This whole story sounded just like delirium in a mental ward. It was like having another mirror that showed the reflection of the previous one. Until that point Vlad thought that the British had a source they could not afford to give away, someone they probably had to cover, and that it was the banker Schumann, however absurd this might have seemed. Clearly, they had to cover up their source with the silent corpse of the agent Smith. Why couldn't this agent Smith have been the source? Yes, he'd expired. Smith had been working with Schumann in the same company at about the same time, and just like Schumann he must have been recruited by the Russians. And this dead body of the agent Smith was supposed to be... Andreas Leman? That appeared all far too clear, too logical, and utterly inevitable. This dead trace, once it was there was like a slight print, inevitably leading to Vlad. Vlad had been paralyzed, in anticipating that this trace would finally hit him. As a matter of fact, he was of no value to the Intelligence, as a mere cross-tie, a cross-sleeper.

And currently this situation had reflected as in a looking-glass, and the trace of Vlad had become mirrored, and it was leading now to a plain office manager Vlad Holt who... How could this man have been an agent? What a lot of rubbish!? Why the trace had taken to him?

And what could have happened, if they had not provided a cover-up for Vlad many years back? I had no wish to consider this, it made me feel nauseated.

I could not to make head or tail of it, was unable to comprehend anything, and then asked,

"Vlad, why could they have needed Andreas Leman as Harvey Smith?"

"There is a case file, with a line on this Smith being settled in Berlin under the name of Andreas Leman. They probably got something else on me on the local records. Information of sorts usually accumulates. However, it looks like they had been given an instruction to let me lie. I've been thinking all this time that they must have forgotten about me, but it's more like they'd deliberately cut off communication with me. Who knows where this case file may be coming from? I was thinking the British may have thrown it up, since there is a clear trace of theirs in this story. They must have known how to devalue this paperwork. Right now the case file looks bogus."

So the Germans had ended up with Andreas Leman for Harvey Smith. Had the Americans known, when delivering Leman to the Germans, that the man could potentially give testify in court? Surely they had known this, yet they had not been ready for the man's visit to the Embassy nor for his confession statement. This had been quite unexpected to all parties. Could it be that the Americans had delivered him so that the Germans could talk to him regarding this confession? This must have looked more convenient.

Vlad was explaining the same to me with a lot of patience, going at an easy pace,

"One can always negotiate things with an agent. Any confession and testimony in court could work in exchange for a mild term in prison. And now imagine, once this guy Michael Brown started talking, it all went to pot, and Andreas Leman turned out to be not a sleeper but a plain business person. What else could they possibly discuss with him? He might be able to act as an agent until the first question came up in court. Who would ever need such a witness? Even the agent Smith twenty years later would not have been more convincing than his corpse. So the British must have wanted to produce in court the corpse of Andreas Leman, which appears a lot more convincing, compared to the living businessman Andreas Leman with the reminiscing about his younger years. The dead man provides a more valid proof."

"Why so...?" I wanted to say, *Why couldn't they have killed Leman right away?*

Vlad had been thinking about it himself, all this time. Why was he still alive? What was the true reason? Could it be due to the fact that Schumann had not been yet been served any charges of espionage? Or was it due to the lack of evidence? Or maybe, Vlad Holt from New York appeared to be a better option, and they had planned to replace Leman with Holt. Michael Brown had just catalyzed the whole thing, and had actually done someone else's job.

The Germans must have learned a while later of Michael Brown's decision to profess that he had been the embassy insider on behalf of the Russian Services, and of the agent Harvey Smith not being Andreas Leman but Vlad Holt. This information could have been intentionally delayed for the death notice of the American Vlad Holt, and that of agent Harvey Smith.

The point was this death of the American Vlad Holt must have been an instant response to the interrogation of Michael Brown, and it was a reflection of the fact that the British were well informed about everything going on in the US Embassy. They probably had an insider of their own planted on site. That is why the banker Schumann had been warned about the pending charges of espionage, and the man had started to look for a convenient witness for himself, and found Harvey Smith.

Vlad had slipped through their fingers, Harvey Smith was still wanted as a witness preferably a dead one and that was why Harvey Smith had been turned into that dead witness.

"These bastards work fucking great. Top performance," Vlad snorted.

Vlad Holt's ashes had been forwarded to dispel any doubts about him being the same person as Harvey Smith. Otherwise why would they have sent them over here? Presumably no one really had any doubts that Harvey

Smith, the man who had disappeared twenty years back, had become an American, Vlad Holt.

Michael Brown had seen this particular person. Brown had lingered for a few days with his confession, and this time must have been enough to eliminate any discrepancies. One could only guess that Brown, just like Vlad, had been for a few days putting down the names of the people possibly affected by his arrest, sorting his paperwork and telling goodbye. This must have been terrible.

Why had it been so easy to mistake the American Vlad Holt for Harvey Smith? Vlad had a single explanation; Vlad Holt must have imitated the work of Harvey Smith. Vlad had assumed this idea and it looked scary to him.

"Vlad, I'm still not getting it. What's the benefit of presenting the ashes of the dead American Vlad Holt in court, and not those of..." I started to say and then paused, Vlad nodded, he knew the answer, but he let me finish my phrase, "...Andreas Leman?"

Vlad started smoking and, still pondering the matter, brushed it aside. In order to properly imitate the agent's work one should have ideally been an agent.

"There might have occurred the following, after a while upon my departure, in order to provide me with the cover, someone might have leaked that the agent Harvey Smith had turned into Vlad Holt in New York... I don't know; it must have been something like that. And then Vlad Holt attracted the attention of FBI counterintelligence. They must have found no evidence, or maybe just some minor details that seemed easy to imitate... It doesn't matter what. Thus, Vlad Holt became known to the FBI as a prospective Russian informant," Vlad was in contemplation lighting up one cigarette after another. "That is why at the moment, now that Vlad Holt has resurfaced as the agent Harvey Smith, no one appeared to have any doubts. Does this sound logical?" he wondered.

Yes, it really looked like a proper false flag. Amazing. By getting Vlad Holt with his long track record, no one could doubt that the man was a perfect fit, so they could go for him.

Leman had eventually survived as there had been evidence linking the agent Smith to the American Vlad Holt. This was just an assumption, but it seemed rather likely.

Who might have given this tip? And when? We would hardly ever get to know this.

Had Vlad Holt been killed? I kept on thinking about it all the time, as killing Andreas Leman to produce his corpse as that of the agent Harvey Smith seemed to be the only easy explanation.

"Holt had been tailored into Smith a long time back. But then that case file came up, and the Americans took on Leman. The British might have allowed those guys to play with Leman a bit, so that after probing the man and holding him in their hands the Americans never returned to him? Leman is a mere businessman, of no interest whatsoever. So that is not the point. We should understand one thing, that is, in what way is this American Holt a better option as the agent Smith than the German, Leman?"

The conversation lengthened, past midnight, and then the darkness gave away, and I left to get some sleep. Vlad was still sitting and smoking as usual, with his elbows on the table, holding his cigarette right in front of his face, and squinting through the smoke. Did Vlad ever sleep? I got accustomed to him having almost no sleep.

Beyond the window it was snowing hard, the gray light looked like twilight, and upon waking up I felt as if I'd had no sleep, this conversation of ours echoing on in my head as though it were endless. Vlad was stood at the doorstep,

"Could you be so kind, could you go shop for the mini cakes and check the cell phone," Vlad requested. "It's time to get up; your coffee is getting cold."

After waking a few blocks away from the house I inserted the SIM card and switched on my cell. I had a message from the lawyer's office of Rivkin saying that Vlad Holt's wife had arrived, and asking me to drop in, in case I was interested in learning of her whereabouts.

CHAPTER FOUR

ILLUSION OF LIFE

Ernest Hoffman was waiting for me at Rivkin's office door. I felt even more chilly looking at his white face. Or was it because I had no idea what to expect from him? Vlad had told me that I had no option but trust the man; actually we had no one else for that matter. Hofmann told me he could give me the address and telephone number of Holt's wife, and offered to have a snack together in a café across the road.

It was somewhat dark inside the café, there was a lamp on the table and its light was splitting the glass facets and spreading them in torn flecks on the white tablecloth.

From outside on the snowbound street the faces of the café guests seemed frozen. A waitress brought us coffee. Hoffmann thanked her with a smile, the way a man thanks a woman who makes clear she likes him.

"Who is she?" I asked him regarding Holt's wife.

Hoffmann told me that I'd better avoid meeting her, not because I was not ready to face her, but because he understood I probably wanted to tell her of my marriage to Holt being essentially non-existent, nothing more than a quick romance at the seaside.

"If you had ever been there," Hofmann said through his teeth sympathetically.

He also added that was all quite understandable, that I must have wanted a quiet life in Berlin. I could have made this marriage a true story but... He wondered if I really wanted to know all. I nodded and he said,

"In a few words, she's not a wife of his and nobody's wife; it's the case where three children are no valid evidence. She's rather clamant," Hoffmann's forehead wrinkled slightly as he frowned.

"She's just an American," I wasn't getting him.

"No, that's not the problem. By looking at you I would think you must cook in silence... My wife... I never know when she's in the kitchen; I can hear not a single plate clank... And this lady would make something of every little thing. I would guess that making a salad takes her a full two hours and everything else in life for her is rather hardscrabble," Hoffmann, running his eyes across my face, noted, "You smoke. Your scarf smells of cigarette smoke. And I actually like you more for it," he said with a faint smile. "So my advice is you'd better not approach this lady. Such women cannot have a husband. I've already told her everything worth saying. I'll give you her hotel address and her phone number, but I hope you've heard me." Hoffmann had a gulp of coffee, wrinkled his lips and added, "I have no idea of what she's doing here, but she probably wants to shred some salad. I'll forward you my office cam shot of hers."

Hoffmann fetched his cell phone, and I took out mine, then caught the reflection of my hungry look in the screen, and a thought crossed my mind, *What if she looks like me?* Something vague but evident to the onlooker? What if I noticed this resemblance and started back from it, like my own reflection in the mirror, where instead of my own face I could see a woman grown old in pursuit of money, an old woman with a young and insatiable glint in her eyes? True, many men escape from such women. Not all of them, though. This kind doesn't want them all; only those who don't escape. I switched on the cell phone and looked at the picture. Well no, there was no similarity, she seemed too rigid, the kind of rigid that red-tapists usually become in their stale offices. In contrast to her I actually looked like a mere rat, responsive and sneaky, able to easily adjust to everything, whatever it was. Were it be a dictatorship or democracy, I would hardly even spot the difference. Sometimes it seemed to me I kept rummaging in my garbage pit, and then at a certain point would just halt and look round, realizing the world had since long changed, and then I would go back to rummaging in my garbage pit.

At the café exit I thanked Hoffmann. Covering my head with the hood of the sand-like powdery snow, I could sense his glance on my back. It crossed my mind he probably had no wife, as waitresses usually had a nose for unmarried gentlemen worth a smile, and he actually had the particular smell of a single man.

When I came back home, after taking out the mini cakes, vodka, cranberry and bockwurst, I passed along that conversation to Vlad.

"Erm, so here we are, we've got the answer as to why this dead American Vlad Holt is better than a dead German, Andreas Leman."

"So why?" I inquired, by catching myself utterly exhausted by yesterday's exchange.

It hadn't been a mere discussion, one couldn't just brush it away, it was something happening right here and now, despite the fact we seemed unable to see through those things. It was just like watching a movie and seeing not the movie itself but its shooting area, while hearing the voices and observing the fuss all around, and thinking of what could have been the costs of the studio rent. The worst part was this film was about us, and yet we could only guess the film script's contents. However, there was no doubt the script itself had long since been written.

"In this case the banker Schumann might have two valid witnesses instead of one. He would have the expired agent Harvey Smith who'd become Holt, and then also a live witness, that wife of Holt's who was able to reconfirm the same. There should be a live witness. This lady must be the British source they could reveal, should the need arise. Does that look like it?"

It held the ring of truth; Vlad was thinking of it no more, he was now thinking of something else. He kept constantly weighing things, and when he was not, he would stand up and leave, and then come back with a carton of mini cakes, some vodka and cigarettes. Every evening, when going to bed, I could see his crooked silhouette over his laptop, or hear his soft steps in the kitchen, all night the light of the reading lamp shinning from under the door crack.

"I find it hard to divest myself of the idea this real Vlad Holt could have been playing the role of Harvey Smith," Vlad told me for yet another time.

"And how do I fucking know what you mean?" I cursed, by feeling a tremendous fatigue wash over me for the fact just yesterday the matter of the ghost of Harvey Smith seemed closed. "Oh my goodness, Vlad, does that mean they had known you used to be not just Harvey Smith and Andreas Leman but also Vlad Holt, who could have known all that?"

Just yesterday Andreas Leman had been only Andreas Leman. It would have been impossible to prove he was Harvey Smith. But with the assumption the real Vlad Holt had been playing the role of Harvey Smith, if Vlad Holt had turned up in court as a dead man, he would make a perfect witness.

Vlad could not say anything for sure; he just shrugged his shoulders in irritation,

"Could you be so kind to make some vodka on cranberry?" he pleaded.

"Vlad, what can be done if this is truly so, and this real Vlad Holt has been posing as Harvey Smith?" I wondered, crashing the cranberry with sugar and pouring vodka into the mesh.

"His information can be set to zero," Vlad replied, as if this were self-evident.

To me it rather sounded like, *We've got here about a hundred kilos of heroin which has to be urgently sold.*

"But how?" I wondered.

"By means of some defector on hire. Could I have more vodka, please?" Vlad requested, and then smiled, looking into my drawn face.

"Vlad, look, you are still alive, and Michael Brown and Vlad Holt are both dead... Don't you think the British lady is taking care of you?" I could sense that Vlad was thinking the same, but could not refrain from asking this question.

"No. I guess she's willing to fuck me to death. I'm so good-looking. And they must have taken that other Vlad Holt from a refrigerator," he added.

"Where from?!"

"See, they don't kill people so fast. The forensic investigator, the paperwork and everything else, one needs some time to get these things done. With that speed they could have only done one thing, open the fridge door. The paperwork must have been ready, with the date of death to be filled in. I have no idea how long he might have stayed in the fridge. For a year? For two years? Or maybe three? As you can see, this is no murder. I've been telling you this, mein herz; so many things only seem true."

"Holt had been in the fridge... And probably for quite a long time. And we just married a year ago."

"But to everyone else he only died a week ago. No one is interested enough to make public he died a while back. And it's rather handy your marriage was solemnized a year ago. This may support the illusion of his life. But whatever way he'd lived and whatever he might have managed to accomplish until his death and thereafter, these things must be set to zero. I'm about to find a solution. Could you stop pestering me? Let us instead find out which Russian bank could have been after this deal of ours. We need a list of some kind, to start with. Would you like some coffee?" Vlad turned his laptop for me to see and got up to make us coffee.

This takeover could only have been orchestrated from Moscow. The invader would not have eliminated Vlad: this seemed not in his interests. They must have wanted the list and not just the list of people as such, but the ways of approaching them. Had they really put enough time into getting to know everyone involved in that deal? Hardly so. Vlad thought that there was a mole in the deal. Until that point the invader had been in a general way knocking out all the partners and middlemen that used to make their payments through Hurst Bank.

Vlad thought that the invader probably needed some more time to realize their mole had not been able to find everyone, and this could keep Vlad safe and secure until the invader received enough information about everyone involved in the scheme.

I remembered asking him,
"Vlad, do you know anything for a fact?"

"I know just one thing for sure. The deal has been sold. There is a mole, probably one of the partners, someone who knows more than others, and who's got information to sell. I can see who it is. The mole fears it. And this is the reason they want to eliminate me. This must be the true reason."

Who could it have been? We still had no idea, with so many unknown variables. That time Vlad told me,

"We actually need to draw one more list... of those who know my face and who are aware of my role in this deal."

Once Vlad had started taking notes, his sheet quickly filled with different names which seemed like a dead end.

"Vlad, you've got one more face," I'd hinted.

"Yeah, fuck, I've got a female face too," he'd said tiredly, looking at me from above his specs, and I'd shuddered.

CHAPTER FIVE

TWO OBLIGATIONS

"...which Russian bank could be after this deal of ours? I don't even have to check that. You won't believe things are that simple... In a word – it's none," I replied.

"None?" Vlad asked me in surprise, by placing a cup of coffee and a mini cake in front of me.

"None. Because no Russian bank whatsoever would ever have enough money, and none would have so much working capital. To have been able to pay for all those years of surveillance and fishing around dirty laundry... It could have only been a major bank in the West, probably hand feeding some Russian bank to cover itself with the same. This Russian bank must be involved with the remission of the Soviet Union's foreign debt. There are even fewer of those that have a good relationship with the Ministry of Finance," I wrote down on a piece of paper some names of banks and arms manufacturing companies. "Let us exclude the Foreign Trade Bank, and also cross out the banks with high government ownership that they can only choke with... Let us then add a couple of monopolists in the arms market that are free to use the secret services as much as they like, and we get three banks and two arms manufacturers. But we should proceed from the fact that no Russian bank has money unless the banker can put his hand into the Minister of Finance's purse, in person..."

"So, let us look at those who have good relationship with the Ministry of Finance," Vlad objected.

"Vlad, the Ministry of Finance is no Fed... it's not a dollar discount store."

"Oh really?" Vlad remarked.

"You must have found something," I guessed.

"Yes, the investigation is ongoing. Look at this," Vlad opened up a newspaper article. "Would you like more coffee?"

"Yeah, thanks," I responded, and froze from a silly thought. "Heh, they've built a case against the Deputy Minister of Finance! Heehee... Vlad, do you think we've been playing games with the government?... Vlad... this can't be true."

"I don't know, I was just thinking. We are already involved in Intelligence games, and not just with a single Service, as you can see...Yeah, this is weird... Why don't we have a call from Victor? I'll get to a pay phone, and find out."

"Vlad, for pity's sake... is your ass burning or what? I'll walk out at night and make the call. I wouldn't be able to manage things without you. Why are you rushing out the door every minute? Are you looking for arrest? You want to dump all of this crap on me at once? The people would scatter away from me as if I had the plague... I should stay with you until they get used to me," I started to moan.

Victor had not called us for a while. Every night around midnight I walked out to make a call to him and check the voice mail of Vlad's company, the way he usually received messages. Otherwise Vlad could sometimes go out. He couldn't keep to the house. The deal itself had been of

Victor's making. It was made up of his contacts and friends, and was his whole life. Victor, after leaving the board of Hurst Bank, had moved to Moscow. He knew that sooner or later the Moscow party would want to get back into the scheme. But who would wish to do so? He had no clue. By living in Moscow he intended to watch out and secure the deal against a hostile takeover.

The moment Vlad had mentioned there might be a defector able to give testimony against him in court, Victor had been ready in a couple of minutes travel bag at the door. Vlad appeared of higher value to him than the whole scheme. He'd left, he'd called us a few times, and then he'd disappeared without leaving his phone number. Why? We could only guess.

"I've been here for two weeks," I could feel irritation in his voice.

"It's not me who's cornered you in here," I hissed at him.

"If Victor were here instead of you, I would have already left this place."

"No. Victor's got no bank. So you are sitting here while Victor frosting up his butt in Moscow in order to arrange a bank for us," I cut him short, and he knew this himself. "I'm sorry; I shouldn't said you this."

"Never mind."

Vlad went to grill the bockwurst. I could smell the sweet fumes of smoke and fat seeping on the wood coal, and felt the warmth of the fireplace in the living room.

The Deputy Minister of Finance had been charged with intentionally forgiving some of the Soviet Union's debts. The arms company West Trade Group was behind the scheme. The Deputy Minister had nothing to do with the matter. It was a stroke against the Minister of Finance. West Trade used to be involved in all those debt deals of the former Soviet Union, and the Minister of Finance had placed those foreign debt bargains into other hands. There was a little war of sorts underway.

"Vlad! Look at this bank here. This is WF Capital Group," I called him.

"Oh, so this must be to whom the Minister of Finance has given the other debt service?"

"This is not about a debt; this is a loan of Russia's. These are two different things. There are obligations of some African countries to the former Soviet Union, the USSR used to be their creditor, they supply their arms in exchange for bananas, and this has been a lasting relationship since long handled by West Trade. The people of West Trade have been sitting in every shitass of this world. In contrast, Russia as a loan debtor must have drawn a loan god knows when, and has been paying it back all this time. And it's because of this particular scheme that the Minister of Finance has told West Trade to get lost."

"Hmm... Russia must be settling the loan not in arms but in ready cash or something else that West Trade hasn't got, then, right? Who has been handling it?"

"WF Capital. Oh, shit! That bank was just founded a year ago!"

"That is, we've got an arms company West Trade Group and then also WF Capital bank, to which the Ministry of Finance had delegated the loan of Russia management," Vlad concluded. "There are two of them, two different banks..." he did not finish.

"And two different interests. In one case this is about money and their trade in weapons, and in the other case this is about pure money and politics. It must be some kind of arrangement, like a wife and a mistress," I made the conclusion for him. "By now Victor should probably know this. Why hasn't he told us? He probably did not expect to stay on. Could he have called us already? Where has he gone?" I almost whimpered.

"Let us wait till the evening," Vlad resolved. "Who's playing against us?"

"The last time, I'm sure it was West Trade acting against us. And they must have got the list of partners in the deal."

"And has this mole stayed with us since how long? How could Victor and I have never noticed him? I've been such an idiot... What can be done?" Vlad started smoking and went up the window.

"Vlad, are you sure all those things underway have not been linked to the deal?"

"Yes, I'm pretty much sure of it," Vlad responded without much thought. "I've told you before: to make me give away the full list of partners in the deal there was no need to call the secret services in, they could have simply beaten up my face, so that I told them everything. Why the hell would they have involved the intelligence forces? No, all this shit must be due to the banker Schumann. I landed there coincidentally. The intruder intending to make the deal takeover must have known about me long ago, and when I'd gotten sucked into this case of the banker Schumann, and the secret services had started all the fuss. When more than a single intelligence service got involved, the intruder probably found himself confined to an auditorium seat. And if he came out, he would immediately be in sight of the secret services, which was highly unwanted."

It crossed my mind, *Oh shit, what is his mind coming up with?*

In the evening I went out to the pay phone. Victor hadn't left us any messages. I bought myself a disposable cell phone and left a message on Victor's voice mail. When I came back, Vlad was still smoking there peering through the half-open window sash.

"Vlad, could we have a mini cake and maybe just rest for a while?"

"Oh, are you now offering me a proper married life? Ten years later the spouses have some mini cakes together while watching sitcom instead of having sex... How could I have ended up in this shit?"

"Vlad, did you ever think that one day you would receive an urn in the mail containing your own ashes?

Take it easy. You would have liked the urn, forgive me, Lord. True, I agree, there's been too much shit happening us and we've been sitting here for quite a long time."

"Oh, we haven't been lying low yet. Now would you like a hut in the snows of Siberia? With potatoes in the frozen earth... What do you think? Where could Victor be?" Vlad wondered, and his face darkened.

"Vlad, I think... we're assuming that the agent Harvey Smith is the American Vlad Holt... He sometimes lived here in Berlin in that apartment of his. But damn it, any of his neighbors, when shown his photo would tell them that this was a different person, that is, Andreas Leman, to be more exact, if they saw the picture of Andreas Leman. How can we possibly avoid it? This is apt to come out. It seems enough that someone just goes around to your neighbors with pictures of the American Holt and Leman and then..."

"I don't give a shit," Vlad brushed it aside. "Andreas Leman is an ordinary businessman. So what if they get to know that I've been using the passport of Vlad Holt, this is mere identity theft. Identity theft is within the jurisdiction of the police and not that of the secret services. I might as well have been selling weed; I wouldn't have sold it under my own name, would I? This is not espionage. I wouldn't really object and could even do without a lawyer."

"And how would you explain bearing the passport of Vlad Holt?"

"I'd say I bought this passport many years ago. We do look similar."

"And who would ever believe it?! Who would play Smith in this case?"

"Holt would do just fine for Smith. He'd lived in Berlin, then left for San Francisco and resided there under the name of Harvey Smith. Upon his return to Berlin, he must have changed his name to Leman, and later on retrieved his old passport under "Holt". This way he'd become more like his former self and would make his way back to New York. May he intended to break off with Moscow?"

"Fuck me gently. And who would ever believe this?"

"There is no need to believe. Holt was born in Berlin, of some common parents and he used to go to school here. If they wish, they can get a photo of Holt in his younger years or his DNA, and then compare things and that's all there would be to it, there would remain only this Vlad Holt. True, he passed himself off as Harvey Smith in San Francisco for a while. Hmm, they must have classified this guy. God damn those Russians, there is no making heads or tails of it. Oh, how simple it used to be for me when I posed as Holt! I was free to stay in bed till late, remained unshaven, and worse the same jacket for years, drinking whiskey," Vlad gave me a blissful grin, but he instantly grew sulky, "You used to have a husband Vlad Holt."

"Should I recognize the man in the photo?"

"No... Not on your life! I'm now pretty much sure they fetched this Holt from the fridge. Oh, damn! How could I have missed it so early in the day! If you recognized him in the photo, that would be the end. Oh, holy crap! So, let us not drink the kind of shit they palm off on us. Do one thing, mein herz; you should find Andreas Leman in the photo. Tell them this person married you using the passport of Vlad Holt. I am no longer the agent Smith but only Andreas Leman. Fuck it. I'll just do my term for identity theft over here. Hoffmann, if he is the person I take him for, probably knows we dwell together with you right here."

"Vlad, listen, and what if they check out the identity of Andreas Leman?"

"Andreas Leman could withstand it," Vlad responded with a faint smile.

"Does that mean, the death did not us part?"

"Right, I'll tell them I married you using a different passport so as to not upset my mother and you've forgiven it."

"Vlad, do I daily see Andreas Leman in you? Or is it somebody else? Who is the real you?" I inquired.

"Not always. Sometimes I get bored with what I am and overextend myself, you know."

"Vlad, and what if the original Andreas Leman shows?" I smiled at him.

"No way. I'd taken a couple of flights and turned up in Thailand, where I'd been forwarded Andreas Leman's passport with which I'd arrived in Germany. Andreas Leman was born in Buenos Aires, after his parents' divorce he lived with his father for a while in Berlin, and later returned to his mother and died. It would have been next to impossible to trace him. Some time later I procured a passport in the name of Vlad Holt. Erm, damn it, I could have made it to Poland or the

Czech Republic, couldn't I? I've been such an idiot," Vlad almost moaned in a low voice.

"Vlad, look, and what if the ashes of Andreas Leman show up this side?" I meant to make it a joke, but then I met his gaze and realized one he had been thinking that move ahead of me.

So how could we possibly arrange things so that Leman would never again turn into Holt? That would have been not as deadly but still pretty bad.

True, Vlad had been living here under the passport of Vlad Holt, but then also Vlad Holt had been using the passport of Andreas Leman for a while. With the assumption, someone had informed Leman of some other man living under his passport, the man had left for Argentina using the passport of Andreas Leman and died there under this name. It would have been impossible to prove the man had committed identity theft from Andreas Leman, had been on the run and had lived with the passport of Andreas Leman for over a month... The man also owned the passport of a German citizen Vlad Holt. And since Andreas Leman had been in conflict with the law in Buenos Aires, the dead guy had perfectly covered up for him. Andreas Leman had started living in these parts with that passport of his; it must have been something like that. Then it turns out that the agent Smith, if he had ever existed, must have died someplace in Argentina.

It looked seamless only in Vlad's words. If only someone could hear it!

"Smith must have died in Argentina, notwithstanding the fact it was the American Holt who posed for the agent Smith in San Francisco, went back to New York and expired just a week ago, really?" I asked him again, doubtfully.

"It was not just a week ago that he died, I can feel it with my ass. Of course, no one is yet aware of this... But then, why couldn't he have died under the name of Andreas Leman in Argentina? It would not really make things any worse for him."

"So, you've been living here with your own passport of Andreas Leman, the one you were born with in Buenos Aires. The American Vlad Holt stole your identity, then left and died in Argentina, and you've assumed his identity and passport..."

"...which I sometimes use. We do look similar. It's rather a temptation one may clearly understand... It's evident to every petty drug pusher," Vlad concluded with a smile.

"But he did not die; in fact, he was living in New York..."

"That was his major problem, but he's got no problems anymore."

"In a word, you are not willing to maintain the illusion of his life the way the British have been doing it..."

"I'd rather set that life of his to zero, I've been telling you this," Vlad replied, turning towards the window.

"But then Leman may easily turn into Smith again..."

Vlad was aware of all those things. Incredible. What was his thinking? He had no wish to be himself, Harvey Smith, it would have been silly; he had not played that man for a while and had long forgotten him. To a lesser extent he was eager to play the dead man Vlad Holt. Whether he wanted it or not, this was not the point. Vlad was actually scared of passing for the defunct Vlad Holt, since the events seemed to be conspiring in such a way that this dead man Vlad Holt could have been the real Harvey Smith. People could believe this story, so it would probably seem authentic. Legends are rather hard to shatter, once created they often fuse with eternity, the reality powerless against the legend.

What was happening? I had become his wife and widow but at the same time we had been staying together all this time in this apartment, from time to time going out to buy mini cakes. All this time we'd been observing the same powder snow falling from behind the window, settling on the roofs and disappearing in the shadow of the neighborhood courtyards, as if it were falling into the water. The evening shadows lit the snow-filled little back yard of ours, filling it up so it seemed more narrow and cramped. In the twilight the snow looked more like frozen water, somewhat milky, and near nightfall it somewhat mixed up with the gray skies, low and blank. The windows of the opposite building were the same kind of black, and by nightfall they reflected the dim light like mirrors, sinking back into their black and void insides. Nothing really changed. This is how the idea of murder could come to your mind, out of nowhere, just because nothing ever changed.

"Vlad, I'd rather kill that banker Schumann and call off this bullshit," I said it the way Vlad used to say things, as if talking to myself, with no expectation of Vlad hearing me.

"Me too," Vlad echoed.

CHAPTER SIX

SET TO ZERO

The cell phone rang beside the laptop, and Vlad instantly grabbed it. Victor had told us we should not expect any calls.

"The bank? Do you know which bank it is?" Vlad asked him in agitation.

"Yes, the bank has been paying off those foreign debts. And they keep knocking off our partners by means of the unwanted list."

"Holt could have passed for me. How can we set this to zero?"

"They'll set it to zero on their own, don't you worry about it," Victor said calmly. "Trust me. You'd better arm yourself with patience."

"What's the bank?" I wondered as soon as Vlad switched off.

We had guessed right, it was WF Capital Group Bank. So we now knew for sure the name of the invading bank.

As to the unwanted list, one could do practically nothing about it. The bank used to get the intermediaries on the hook. The unwanted list was a smooth-running scheme normally used by the FBI, which worked as a conveyor; one only had to fill in the desired names. The FBI using its own facilities closed in on the functionaries for which they had incriminating evidence, and then suggested to them that they to give away either some of their colleagues or the Americans suspected of corruption. Some of these people agreed, some refused. The surnames of the corrupt officials used to be prompted. The FBI filled up their list, and those who agreed to cooperate were instantly covered by the witness security program. Those who refused were subtly denied bank accounts or entry to the USA. The appointments in question were usually held some place abroad, in a quiet country, the kind of Sweden.

That way, the suspect list of money laundry and criminal links was got replenished, with this list was intended for the banks. The banks would deny the people on the list, using various excuses, from opening any new bank accounts and would probably close off their old ones. This way the list filled in with the names of the deal participants.

How many of them could WF Capital have identified? We had no clue. How could WF Capital have come to terms with the FBI? God only knows. But because the FBI had much to gain from it, there were probably no questions. The list kept growing, and the common recruiting agents received their bonuses, why not?

The bank itself was a ghost from nowhere. There was not a single familiar name on their board; the bank had neither funds nor property. The bank was in charge of the loan service, the loan drawn by Russia many years ago with some Asian and Arab countries.

Why this obscure unheard-of bank? The answer was not so complicated. Russia kept settling this loan using hard cash and some political concessions. That is why this bank appeared to be the invader.

"Vlad, I've got a feeling this bank has been intentionally created to the takeover of this deal of ours. Does it seem likely?"

"Too much likely," Vlad replied, and this made me feel uneasy.

How funny, the things Vlad was telling me intertwined in some intricate ways with the events underway past the walls of this house of ours. His words seemed to be pulling in the reality.

"Vlad, I'm afraid they could be playing this card with Harvey Smith not for the court against Schumann, but for you. If Vlad Holt had been in the fridge biding his time, that means someone's known about you and the deal for quite a while," I caught myself asking this question for the third or fourth time already, yet Vlad always seemed to have no answer.

"No. I've been telling you they don't really need all those ins and outs to just get me knocked out of the scheme. True, they knew things for a while, but these actually had nothing to do with the deal itself. This crap is to be sorted into several piles; I've been telling you this. There must be something else. Something we did not notice right from the get-go because... I've been really scared. Initially I didn't have a clue," Vlad responded, starting to smoke.

"Do you think the banker Schumann is really so important?"

"They don't really fuck around. The deal might have come into view of the British Intelligence by chance. In other words, until now I have never seen the British Intelligence so flat-out. And at this point it rather looks like we are sorting out who spreads for whom," Vlad screwed up his face. "Look, the banker Schumann is getting covered by the British Intelligence. This is evident. Do you think they had started protecting him just a month ago? No way. This kind of cover-up operation might take years of work. They must have made Vlad Holt an agent recruited by Moscow long ago, or maybe, it was not of their making, and they could have just supported that legend. And upon the man's death they must have put him into the fridge."

"Vlad, why would they need this legal action against a banker whose bank is the size of a dog-hole?"

"It may have been the same as that blow against the Deputy Minister. The man may have nothing to do with it, and this is a mere warning to the Minister of Finance. The banker Schumann seems to be a target for hire. There may be someone behind the man, someone of higher value, someone, who must be the real target that Schumann is about to cover up for. I don't really know."

Vlad told me they might have been keeping Schumann in view for years, collecting the information little by little. Since it had come up for legal action, this meant that the two parties had failed to come to terms in a peaceful way. In most cases it was a political set-up job. They must have required this court action against the banker Schumann for purposes that involved political matters. The Americans must have been collecting the data on Schumann for quite a long time. In this case either the Americans had been too hasty, so the evidence turned out to be insufficient, or they had fallen into the trap of the cover story prepared for Schumann by the British.

They must have been making arrangements for that covering operation for a long time. There must have been some trace of it, or repercussions for a while before all this fuss with Schumann. And the dead body of Vlad Holt must not have been the only master card they'd possessed. There must have been something else, for sure.

"Vlad, I'm not getting a thing with this American Holt."
Vlad didn't have a clue himself, all he had was his guesswork,
"I guess someone had wanted to protect me, a long time ago. I told you earlier, I might have met a big man, and then a few years after my departure the man must have come into sight. I have not been sitting idle. The Russians sidetracked attention from me by tipping-off that the agent Smith was American Vlad Holt. The question at issue is, how long have they known about me living under the name of Vlad Holt? I have to admit they must have known this for a while. Who would have ever needed to find out things about me, if they'd plain forgotten about me since my arrival in Berlin, and no one even tried to contact me, as if they'd put a lid on me for good? Shit, I've been so sure they had forgotten all about me. But then maybe, when the person I used to date become too visible, they must have felt constrained to divert suspicion from him. The idea to get on the track to this American Holt could have shot into someone's mind,

couldn't it? Suppose this Holt had come to the attention of the FBI counterintelligence. They must have found nothing and just put freeze on the matter..."

"Vlad, is that at all possible? That is, to suspect a man of espionage and then back off? What do you mean, back off? The FBI? FBI would probably back off once they drove the man to the grave... or put him into the freezer."

"There is no evidence. Over the years it sometimes occurred that the man working for the Russian Intelligence was in charge of just a single task, reporting to no one really, so he could continue living his own life. They could just as well continue tracing him for another ten or twenty years, all in vain. And this was generally well known, so they could have backed off."

"Really?" I could not believe this was possible.

"Erm, there can be sometimes a fictive agent. Let us assume an FBI agent upon receipt of a tip-off to Holt had made the decision to work with the man. It actually happens this way. He must have assisted Holt in meeting some people, by pushing and challenging him, and then finally the agent himself must have fallen under suspicion of being a highflier, who just needed that harmless clerk Holt in order to get his own promotion. This must have been somewhat more difficult to arrange but still possible. Later on, the British must have learned of this Holt and increased the interest in the man. This is how the cover-up operation for the banker Schumann must have started."

"How could one possibly increase the interest?" I asked him.

"They may have thrown some evidence to the agent in charge of Holt's case, so he'd turned to the case again. I have no idea. We are free to think anything we want."

"But that Holt, as an agent, must have been doing something, say, handing over some paperwork or at least collecting it from someone else."

"True. This is something to be set to zero."

"What if he'd been used? If they had already known of him, he might have been handing over whatever, you name it."

"Exactly. I'm not going to miss out on that."

"And what about that banker Schumann? What if the legend of the agent Smith busts, and the man would never be able to get out of court?"

"He would. As you see, there is so much information surrounding him; it had taken much time to provide him with the cover. Just forget him. By the way, Schumann, to my mind, is some kind of disposable agent. He had not even changed his name. He used to work for the audit firm under his own surname and then later arrived in Berlin under his own surname. This kind of person would not normally arouse any suspicion, unless someone had told something to someone credible which they must have believed."

"Vlad, may I ask you another silly question? And what was your job in the audit firm? It seems weird."

It did seem weird. Or did I not know chalk from cheese?

Vlad's firm had been servicing several companies created by the Russians in order to imperceptibly buy up their foreign debt and its privately owned share in the open market. These companies were all kinds of businesses, with the majority of them IT companies, easy to pump in and siphon off money. The auditor surely knew how all of these funds were applied, and the companies had no links to their owners.

"Hmm... and what if this Schumann had taken my place in the company? A single time is enough," Vlad seemed taken aback with that guess, I could see him find the clue himself, but he preferred not to tell me.

Set the whole thing to zero. How could that possibly work out? It could touch the people Vlad had been linked with, it was about their lives. What impact would it have on them all?

In fact, Vlad told me that we had to eliminate all corroded elements in this scheme of ours. Indeed, I couldn't help agree that it was high time to get rid of certain partners, and in particular, some of the middlemen to the deal. Could we just give them away to the counterintelligence? Factually, we could do so, and Vlad surely had a point there. It seemed workable. So maybe one day I could drop in for a cup of tea at Hoffmann's place. In this scheme the people used to receive nothing but money.

But the Intelligence was a different setup where many things were done without seeking a profit. In fact, its making was most often destroyed, as it really happened quite a bit. And surely, the people were ready for this. However, to set up to zero everything in connection with Harvey Smith, actually meant demolition of everything those people had been doing and not for a living for years. Vlad would turn into a traitor. Was this something he truly wanted? For better or worse, this appeared the best of a bad bunch of choices in store for him. He might have already been a dead traitor. And when people have choice, they prefer to be left alive rather than die.

True, making Vlad Holt out of him was a kind of treachery too, but it was that of the system, and was therefore somewhat easier to forgive while. The treachery of a single man could not be forgiven.

Or could I have gotten it wrong?

"Vlad, you would be a traitor and destroy lives. Or is there something I fail to understand? At least, we've gotten to know well what exactly you are about to destroy."

"True, surely I wish to know that. I'm going to make a call to a friend of mine. I guess they replaced Harvey Smith with Vlad Holt because to him, actually ... By the way, if they had outperformed so that I was left alone for twenty years, then..." I could see his gaze freeze, "There must be a second case file."

"A second case file? Could it be that way?"

"No. However, when trolling for a mole any jig will do. So Holt must have been a jig for someone else. I may be wrong, and Holt might have managed to do not as much as the agent Smith. One doesn't need to do much really. He must have diverted attention. And once he'd attracted more attention than necessary, they must have killed him."

"Killed him, you know."

"No no. That urn must not have contained the ashes of Vlad Holt," Vlad noted.

"But whose?"

"No idea. Why would they have burned it, if they could just as easily use it again? They might as well send over one more urn with the ashes of Andreas Leman, so that I'll die as Andreas Leman. That would really hurt. I've got so many close friends. That has been my real life. I could hardly survive my own death; I'm not an Iron Man. And then, after all those events I wouldn't really hasten to get rid of his body. By the way, the man probably has my teeth. I haven't been hiding, just been living a common life, visiting my dentist and paying my parking tickets... Fuck, this corpse will haunt me until it drives me to the grave," Vlad cussed out. "And the wooden stake would be of no help. In a word, wherever I go and, whatever passport I take – oops, the corpse with my own face and teeth is waiting for me."

"But then, looking at him you will see yourself free of all those by-gone issues. Oh my goodness, Vlad! All these things... it's not my cup of tea, all this delirium ad infinitum. That's not my own bullshit. I've had enough of my own. This is far too much."

"Oh, don't you freak out. It was just an assumption. I've started thinking that way. And you've been thinking the same, do you remember? Shit, it all seems rather logical. You see, I'm not thinking to set everything to zero. I'm just willing to keep that dead man from haunting me. For that matter, I'll need that surname, Holt. Do you mind marring me, mein herz?" he asked me with a smile. "I'll get you a mini cake. And then you could bury me again. That sounds interesting, so how many lives could I have?"

"They'll kill me, and that'll be a perfect way to stop all that nonsense."

"I'm so tired of you being silly," Vlad sighed and turned away, resting his eyes on the black and white roof lines over the window. "No, this is no fault of yours; I've driven myself to this kind of thinking on my own. This is the reality, there is no fiction. This was no cheap thrill. This is all about big money that someone already invested into the deal takeover. Is that clear? Try to think like a financial expert, there are moneymen playing against us. And all this funeral fuss is showing support from the secret services. The intelligence guys are not the decision makers, they are just getting paid for their assistance, and they work the best they can, those whorechildren. They don't kill; they just wreck your life. They may arrange a custodial arrest for you, some time in prison with no right to bail. Murder is not their style. Could you please make it so that I never hear that bullshit again from you?"

"Vlad, we aren't yet married and you're already making up a family quarrel. What am I supposed to think when you say this dead man will keep haunting you? And what about Vlad Holt? Haven't they killed him already? The story of them putting him into a fridge must be a mere fabrication by your mind," I almost let it slip, *Of that sick mind of yours.* "Let me be a widow of yours for a while, okay?"

"You can leave if you wish. You are free to get back to your own life any time. Anyways, could you take care of the bank? We do need a bank, mein herz," Vlad said in a softer tone. "Are you on the deal?"

What was this fucking world?! I'll never be able to understand the logic of it, I cussed silently and started to smoke. *Damn good-looking. How can I refuse if he says he'll get me a mini cake? The hell with it, I'll keep fighting for this deal till the last client.* And I said out loud,

"I'm in the deal. I've been looking for the deal that could make my life, whatever it is... But I hadn't known there would be a blonde as a bonus ... Yeah, I'll be in to the bitter end. And you know that."

CHAPTER SEVEN

MIDDLEMAN

Within these two days I seemed to lose Vlad. Out of sight, he was back to making the lists of those who were apt to come into view, in case his true identity had been leaked. He took out his sheets, crossed out some names, and then put down new ones. We suggested that if the whole story regarding the American Vlad Holt returned to zero, then it would probably get back to Andreas Leman, who had later turned into Vlad Holt, and we could get overwhelmed by this great wave of bullshit once again. I did not ask whether it was possible to set all of it to zero. It was out of the question.

The first name on the list was Maximilian Richter. Vlad had put down this name long ago, and it was on top of several lists of his.

"Vlad, you aren't the decision maker at this point. Leave it to the people for whom any association with you might prove costly. It would cost Richter his career."

"No, mein herz, it would rather cost him his life. I don't know."

"Vlad, why don't you want to just leave everything the way it is? Why couldn't Harvey Smith be Vlad Holt, the man that died in New York? It would have no bearing on you. You would just remain Andreas Leman."

"Something tells me the harmless corpse of this office clerk might conceal a pretty deep grave of a fucking lot of bullshit. Can't you see it? This Vlad Holt is an outhouse, where they've dumped all that crap of mine; they must also have dumped yet another load of crap there. That second case file," Vlad cussed. "Is like creating a new man. There is none, so he could sustain whatever they would pile on him. I have no wish to be one. And I don't really fancy that wife of his."

In the morning Vlad told me to make a call to Richter, to request an appointment of a couple of minutes and brief him on everything he might be interested in knowing. He surely needed to know all, so that he could protect himself. If it got out he'd been familiar with Vlad, it would have cost him dearly. He was a counsel at law with an office in New York and another one here in Berlin, his law firm Richter&Koch was in the phone directory. I had to present myself as Vlada Holt, he knew the name. If Richter was in Berlin, he would most probably make an appointment at the airport cafe. I could be fortunate to catch him out on this side.

"Vlad, shouldn't we wait a bit for a call from Victor?"

Vlad gave me a nod,

"We've got to hurry up. Victor is working alone; he won't have time to find out all the details. Yes, that friend of mine has been working for everyone; hope he is still a friend. Go."

It got warmer but there was still no sky to be seen, it was there but it seemed totally bare, explicit and bald, all of it evenly lit with measured gray light. The snow kept melting, spreading out along the roadway and the footpaths, by catching the dim light and welding with the void of the skies. From afar the high-risers seemed ice-bound, and the city itself looked somewhat nude and frozen in the cold wind.

In the café I asked for the phone directory, and dialed the number of the lawyer's office,

"Maximilian Richter, please. This is Vlada Holt. It's private."

They put me through right away without asking any questions. And quickly, before I could say anything, a heavy low voice asked me,

"Are you there?"

"Yes."

"I'll be soon in the airport. You could find me in the café," and he hang up.

Maximilian came to me in no time and pressed on my shoulder to make me sit by his side at the café table. The man was in his sixties, with a rigid as if frozen face that looked like a crumpled white shirt pinched by cold, every line around his lips seemed to have broken up and then hardened, as if his traits had been totally accomplished, as if he had chosen this face for himself. The gaze of his gray eyes seemed clear and settled, and when looking into his eyes, I caught myself unwillingly thinking that he must have murdered a couple of clients of his just before breakfast. He probably was a perfect counsel at law. Oh God, I felt so easy and comfortable with him...

"Could you tell me in few words of whom we are talking here?"

"He does not like shaving and he has a scar under his chin," he stopped me with a gesture, asking,

"What happened?"

"The British lady's mucked up."

Strangely enough, this phrase of the Russian Chancellor Gorchakov was still well remembered, even if he used to live in the nineteenth century. Richter nodded,

"Get to the point."

I said Vlad had been in control of the foreign debts buy-up scheme, and it seemed to be on the verge of takeover by a Russian bank, which by having all those debts in hand probably found it easier to pay off their own debts to some Asian countries.

"And you?" he wondered, clearly understanding things, in disbelief.

"I'm his backup. Believe me; I should not have been here. There originally must have been a different person in my place. But all of it went to the dogs in a split second."

"The turnover?" he inquired, nodding.

"Hurst Bank. We've lost it. The deal is on freeze. That is due to him having worked twenty years back for the same company with the banker Schumann. The investigation is ongoing. They wish to have a dead witness. They've sent over the ashes of the American Holt who was supposed to pass for the dead witness, agent Smith. This can be reconfirmed by his wife."

"How have they found him?" his question referred to Vlad.

I told him there must have been a case file, and we guessed it probably contained an old photo and the name of Andreas Leman. Everything had been heading in that direction that Andreas Leman was to make a dead witness. Leman had managed to bluff it out. But the Embassy translator had been a middleman to the deal, so he'd identified him as Vlad Holt. And they'd instantly sent the ashes of Vlad Holt, the American, masking as the ashes of Smith. I told him that Vlad was sure of that this American Holt passed for Smith. Yet this single suspicion seemed enough. Someone had faced off the threat of Smith by taking it to the American Vlad Holt.

"Hmm, does he really think I could have been the reason? That is, they covered up for him due to his contact with me..."

"He has no idea as to how much this Holt might have told them as Smith. He would rather have it set to zero," I responded.

Maximilian considered this for a moment.

"I am not ready to die. But then, if the British... How long could the British lady whore have known about the deal?"

"She did not really know."

"Then she would rather set it all to zero on her own, unless she's a dumb Dora," he concluded, getting on his feet.

He said he would try to find out as much as he could, and suggested someone else should give him a call in a couple of days.

"Victor. He'll give you a call," I answered.

"What have you been before?" asked Maximilian, glancing at his watch and running his eyes across my face, as if something important was left unsaid.

"A trader."

"Very good. Then you'll get it. You've got freckles, I haven't noticed before," he noted while resting his vacant eyes on my face. "I want you to forward something to him. Follow me quickly, don't stop."

Richter pushed me slightly and headed at a lively pace towards the toilets. Even quicker he opened the door to the men's room, let me through, and quickly entered himself, shouldering me into the cubicle, and turning my back to the wall, gently holding my throat as he gave me a kiss, softly pressing his lips hot with coffee to mine. This affection of his overwhelmed my whole body with a hot wave of desire. In a second he got off. I ran away similarly hot, but he was nowhere to be seen. As I approached the exit I recollected that I had been a trader all my crazy rough-and-tumble life, and it crossed my mind,

This son of a bitch just cut ten years off me, thus setting it to zero in a split second.

Vlad was waiting for me at the stairway. He was smoking and his cigarette smoke not blending with the icy air kept falling away.

"Vlad, he'll find out as much as he can. He also thinks this might be due to him."

I told him about our meeting. Strangely enough, I thought that Vlad would ask me about Maximilian's looks. It was a good thing he never asked this question, I had no idea what to say. For me, Maximilian looked rather like a veteran killer; he had the charisma of someone who easily crossed far over the boundaries.

Could have Vlad forgotten him? Or was he just too exhausted these days? I believed it was impossible to bring anything back, and when parting the people had better part ways for good, as the past could never return in the same old way. We tend to think of the past as being better than it actually is, and by accidentally facing it we give ourselves pain, for the past is a deception. I had seen Victor strive to regain his wife, he must have been aware it was impossible, but he still wished to have her back. He had known everything and still preferred to make sure there was no way back.

We moved to the kitchen and I stopped Vlad by holding his arm, *Vlad, Maximilian was asking me to tell you this,* I pushed him into the toilet, turned him about by holding throat. He understood, sliding slightly down the wall, and closed his eyes for a second. I had not known we could actually pass on a kiss. It was not really me there. It was the power of love, that of true love capable of growth like a tree. I ran out. The door closed.

With age sex may be different, like a book read through. I remembered meeting Ilya for the first time. Ilya used to smell of snow, but maybe that was the fragrance of his cologne, or that of his house, of his white chair slips and his crumpled bed sheets, or that of the white window curtains. Coming up to his house I found it hard to shake off the feeling of snowfall in that house of his.

Ilya had asked me then,

"Whom would you like to sleep over with, me or my security team?"

I had been hardly able to respond,

"You never know who you may land in bed with, in these hard times, do you, Ilya?"

He said,

"Don't be silly. We're already done over with you, it's already happened."

The moment I had become Vlada Holt, even hardly opening the passport, to my mind this life of mine had changed for good. For one second I had felt free to set that passport aside, back into the envelope, and thus preserve my life the way it used to be with Ilya. I had not really wanted any other life. I'd feared ruining everything. But the time had come to change it. Why was it up to me? I wanted to get somewhat closer to Ilya, which meant I was about to change something. It seemed fair to take that risk.

"Could you bring the cigarettes over here, please?" Vlad requested.

I handed the pack and the lighter through the half-open door without looking, and said I was going to leave a message to Victor, for him to contact Richter.

Upon my return I found Vlad smoking in the kitchen, the ashtray beside him was full.

"Vlad, how are you?" I inquired.

"Did they been told you as a kid not to take any sweets from male strangers?" Vlad wondered, without looking.

"Is that about Richter? He was asking me what I had been before. A trader. And they usually thrust onto the trader whatever turns up so fast you have no time to decline. Vlad, well, he might have had another two or three minutes, what difference would it make? It actually has nothing to do with me. I'm just your backup."

"For real? Would you hookup with him in the men's room?" I could sense the mockery in his voice.

"I've got no wish to play the fucking backup," I snapped and added in a softer tone. "Vlad, there's too much affection in him; he must have accumulated so much over years. He wasn't looking into my eyes, he just glanced at my freckles. I would have noticed if he'd really liked me. Are you jealous?"

"That makes no sense, he fucks whatever comes his way," Vlad waved it away, yet I could see he was telling this just for me.

"But he loves you. Why don't you stay with him?"

"And why don't you stay with your own husband instead of sitting here with me? I can't really ditch my life to just be with him. You see me as good-looking just because you know so little of me. I'm no good-looking. He does not want me that way."

It crossed my mind it was all nothing but fairy tales, they come to love us the way we are, but we'd better not believe it. Ilya wanted everything from me, all I was able to do and all I wasn't, making me seek him, so I was there with him. I did not really want the man to appreciate me the way I was. I didn't really fancy myself the way I'd been. I wanted to be something different for Ilya. Yet I had no time. Ilya was far advanced in age. What if I'd missed the right time? Would I be able to forgive myself? Not too ago I had been thinking that if only Ilya wished so, he would have told me he wanted to see me daily. And now I knew he had not told me this, because I had been unwittingly putting him off. I'd been putting off the only man of my life. Why so? Was it because I'd been willing to be in time for something? And had I been wasting this time of ours, of which there was not so much left? One day Ilya would be fed up of waiting for me to be done with tickling my own ambition. Or I would get back to him far too late. So what could I do? How could I be everywhere at once?

"You're right. This is this fucking life of ours, and we've chosen it that way. Let us make it sweet then. Have we got any mini cakes left?"

"And vodka. I should have a drink now. So have you had a fuck or not?" he asked me again after a gulp of vodka, his lips tightly pressed, and I could see he had already had a few, so he'd better not ask that question.

"Vlad, there are over a hundred partners in the deal. Don't you tell me you hadn't hooked up with any of those? I've seen that man looking at you, the one with hollow cheeks..."

"What?"

"Like a cat around hot milk."

"Shit happens," Vlad admitted.

"Why would I lie? I'm not a lawyer. You could ask him yourself. Or you can think what you want. It still hurts him, he probably wanted to tell you this," it flashed through my mind. "Vlad..."

"What?"

"You didn't know that."

"I didn't really want to know, I feared to."

CHAPTER EIGHT

OLD BOMB

Victor left me a message to come and meet him at the airport. Looking back at Vlad in the doorway, I intended to tell him I'd be back soon or something like that, but I failed. What could I tell him? Vlad had been exhausted by all this anticipation, by expecting the unknown.

I walked out again into the gray downtown, the sky looked reversed and the sun was hardly shining through, it seemed a mere reflection in the dim water. I thought this city kept pulling me in sure as death.

Victor came up very soon. What a relief it was to see him there! When I received no calls from him I felt really scared, it felt as though he would never be able to call again.

Who would have ever thought ten years earlier Victor had been a respectable German citizen, a board member on Hurst Bank?

Victor in and of himself was a robust and mature boar in his sixties, wearing an expensive suit worn-out to one cent and impregnated with a cheap cigarette smell. His face with its massive features looked swollen more than ever, as if loosely caked over the wintertime. His hair was touched with silver, and his dark eyebrows closed up to the nose bridge with a few deep furrows cutting across his forehead. He had sunken pale eyes surrounded by dark circles, and his broken somewhat crumpled lips usually screwed even further as he smiled.

"Hi, bunny," he eagerly took a step towards me and gave me a hug.

"Victor, oh gosh, I thought I'll never be able to see you again."

"I've got to leave. Let us change the communication means," he gibbered, and gave me the phone numbers of two different firms where he could leave us a message. "If I don't make a call, don't worry. I've seen Richter and also had time to find out a few things

126

myself," he motioned me a sign to keep silent, and said he would first tell me what he'd been able to find out.

Victor pulled a cup of coffee closer to him and gulped, then habitually felt in his pocket for the cigarettes, and spitting out an oath fished out a vape, and grumbled, *It looks like a dildo from a sex shop,* before putting the damn thing aside.

He said something was underway on the American side, as if an invisible bomb had exploded; they had noiselessly started some check-ups and layoffs. It felt like the bomb had been planted twenty years back, to go off just recently by mistake. Right now they seemed to be after a group of Russians that had been involved in San Francisco and New York. The unit had been discontinued since long but not in the usual way. Some of the team members had been covered up. Vlad had a second case file.

"Vlad has actually guessed there must be a second case file," I nodded.

"Yeah, I could not believe it. It may have been due to the sleeper. The sleeper must have been searching for the people who had been recruited the same way as Smith, at about the same time. They must have provided for two different case files not just for Smith alone. They must have got the paperwork done and slipped them in. As for the second file, Holt had left Berlin for San Francisco as Smith. This case file must be older. To find out this German Holt is, in fact, the American Holt is rather easy. The man has his parents in these parts, he'd attended his school here... so they already know."

"Victor, would anyone be able to spot the counterfeit?"

Victor said the forged file was of high quality, that kind of paperwork was usually ordered from Czechia, from the craftsmen of unit eight working with the First Directorate. These people were capable of making any document of whatever contents and age.

"But then someone must have procured the initial case file. Otherwise they would not have learned that Smith had turned into Leman. Who could have got a hold of it?"

Victor had no idea. In his opinion, this first case file had been kept by the Stasi. What could have been the options for the British lady with that case file and a dead witness ready to serve? Could they have succeeded in making everyone believe in this file being a counterfeit? No, the more you try to convince people, the less they trust what you say. The British know how to pervert other people's ideas in their own way, which appears far more secure than to argue with the obvious. And they had actually succeeded in doing so. Despite the case file's existence the ashes of Holt were considered to be those of Smith.

"That is, have the Germans passed over the case file? We've thought all this time the Germans don't really want any spy scandals..."

"There seems to have been no choice, otherwise, the case file would have been considered of no value twenty years after."

I had some more questions to ask but Victor stopped me, he was pressed for time.

"I met a person who had seen Holt earlier in New York. He'd become a defector living in Boston. The man's a bit inadequate... I mean he seems fine, he does not wear any black sunglasses and has no intention of writing his memoirs, yet he is self-destructively obstinate, like of Vlad. These guys don't survive."

The man had been under suspicion. They had directed him to Holt. What could have happened with Holt? It remained unclear, but the man could not have refused to visit him. They might have given a word to the FBI, or the FBI might have learned it a bit later. In fact, this defector had come to talk to Holt. After a couple of words he must have understood that he'd been talking to the wrong man, so it had been a trap. Could he have wished to kill this Holt? God only knows. He might have wished to do so. Holt had gone missing soon after. Nothing had really happened; pure zero.

That time, per the man's initial thinking, with Holt being dead, since he used to be an agent, someone was supposed to take care of the matters left undone until the news of his death got leaked. Why not? And currently the man had gotten to thinking that Holt's wife must have killed him. It seemed irrelevant and at this point impossible to find out. However, it mattered because the man could be accused of Holt's death. He'd been kept on the hook. It had been suggested that he play a witness in court and reconfirm that Holt had been actually Smith. But this also meant to admit that he would have had a motive for killing the man. Would he be able to sustain and turn down that proposal? That remained unknown.

"And the main thing is, when he was shown the photo of Leman, he told them this was not Smith, as a matter of ordinary care. In a word, we've been lucky the man did not throw caution to the winds," Victor concluded.

Victor had found no one else capable of passing for a witness in a court process against the banker Schumann.

What was all this bullshit? I could not tell what it looked like; it was rather an invisible chain linking all kinds of people. At an early phase I had not considered it to be a chain, as it resembled the stock market in crisis with everyone sick and delirious and passing it all on to others. Right now it was looking rather like some dirty laundry, with the linen being passed from hand to hand where the more hands touched it the cleaner it became.

At this particular moment the woman in charge of Holt's wife role was about to wash herself clean, with her dirty linen thrown over to the defector who had once seen Holt in person. Into whose hands might this linen get passed further on?

"Vlad was thinking they might have sidetracked Smith's suspicion because of Richter. But then, could Holt have posed as Smith in some way or another?"

Vlad had guessed it right. Victor told me it sometimes happened if a recruited agent was of high value that; the people informed of his recruitment would be called off to the country to prevent any unwanted leaks. Richter used to be that kind, so Smith had been sent over to Berlin and then his communication had been totally cut off. His meeting with Richter in Berlin had been a mistake; luckily, it had not lasted for long. There must have been some other people.

True, it had been already known that Smith had taken the passport of Holt in addition to that of Leman. They must have diverted suspicion about Smith, so the American Holt had come out.

Initially Holt had attracted attention as a prospective agent, nothing else. The man used to have a wife and three children. He'd been living a common life. Someone must have told his wife they'd seen him in Berlin with a man, with a photo, yet we could never tell at what point she might have started thinking her husband had been recruited. Anyway, she must have told to some counterintelligence agent about her husband. It must have been private, since the man used to be a friend of hers; she'd just wanted to know. What might the latter have learned? There was nothing but suspicion, which was not enough to launch an investigation, yet was enough to break up Holt's marriage.

Or otherwise there must have been some other reason for it.

So Holt had remarried, and his second wife had managed to arrange so that his children could stay with them. This had happened three years back.

Victor had no information as to whether they had been trying to make the agent Smith out of this Holt. It might have just been sufficient to have him as a sleeper. Everything had been done by that wife of his.

"Vlad thinks they took that Holt out of the fridge, then filled in the date of his death and forwarded his ashes up here."

"Yes, I'm about to find out. It looks like Holt went missing three years ago."

"Victor, I'm afraid that in the course of this research you might..." I didn't finish my thought.

"That is why in case I don't come through, don't worry about me."

"Vlad feels bad that the deal has been scuttled due to him. Couldn't they have found someone else to cover the ass of that banker Schumann?!"

"The hell with the deal, I'd rather not lose Vlad, these guys could make him a dead witness any minute now. Tell him to keep the house. You should not contact anyone else. He's taken too much risk with Richter. Vlad has been putting Richter at risk, so everything may go up shit creek. I've told you I'll take care of it all. I'll be making calls to Richter sometimes, he's a counsel at law, it would be easy for him to find out what's there in court, and when the action gets started. That's the main point. Vlad is not supposed to set anything to zero with his own hands. Let them do it for him. I'm sure they would, I just feel convinced, everything seems to be going that way, I cannot tell you now, and I've got no clue. I understand you'll now be eliminating the excessive middlemen. Feel free to do so, the deal is Vlad's territory so he probably knows what has to be done. But this court battle, hell only knows whose territory it is. Could you hold Vlad back? Let him first find out the smallest details before doing anything."

"Could Vlad have a reason, and this Holt had been kept in the freezer all this time?"

"Yes, why not, if there is such a witness as this wife of his, an experienced agent? Look, Richter procured the correspondence of Holt's wife for three years," Victor passed me a pen drive. "They've got it disclosed for the legal proceedings. It was actually written for them to see. It's so touching. We can see the cover-up operation for Schumann had been getting ready for three years. Holt went missing right away."

"Victor, we sort of married just a year ago. Vlad told me I should identify the man in the photo not as Holt but as Leman. And it's rather risky to recognize Leman in the picture. I guess Vlad is right. But then... Victor, we've got to give our own version of Smith's death. If they start checking up with the neighbors of the German Holt, they would not recognize him from the photo but would identify the man as Leman. Could it be so that Leman, upon his discovery that someone else had been using his passport, made inquiries and learned that Smith had left for Buenos Aires with his passport and died there...," I did not finish as Victor cut me short,

"Don't you start doing someone else's job, bunny. They must be already working on this. They are quite professional. Enough to pin them down to facts doggy-style, and they'll think it through."

Victor stood up and quickly headed for the flight registration counter. I trotted by his side, asking,

"The British stand by Schumann. Why so?"

"There must be many reasons. He must be the money box. He is a smart son of a bitch; he must have amassed enough compromising material and should be sleeping a peaceful sleep by now."

"Schumann has not changed his surname. He's a common businessman. What might he have?"

"Vlad had better find out. Must be something from the old days."

"He probably knows but does not tell me. Why have do I have the feeling the British lady is patronizing Vlad?"

"Must be for that reason. I was also thinking earlier they were about to make Vlad into a dead witness. However, you see, there's already been a dead witness... Well, catch you later, bunny," Victor threw his arms around my shoulder, and I burrowed my face into his coat which smelled of cigarettes and something else, either rain or melting snow, the fragrance that always stayed with him. It was the smell of Moscow.

I wondered what could be there in that correspondence of hers? Upon my return I opened up the emails in the pen drive, and called Vlad,

"Vlad, have a look here."

Everything looked like the usual family life, some doubts, suspicion, lies and cheating. Three years back Holt was said to be thinking about suicide, while she fondly believed she'd pulled him out of those glum thoughts, and onto feeling happy and needed, but the man seemed to retrace this train of thought again and again. She guessed he had arrived at these ideas not of his own accord, but from something in his past must have been pushing him towards this way of thinking. The man looked devastated. Her initial thinking was the daily routine was killing him, and then she realized that he must have been expecting termination of employment due to downsizing, yet this fear was different, he seemed to be struggling to escape. Then she asked him, why he wouldn't visit a couch doctor. He refused. One day he asked her, whether she wished to live somewhere nearby a forest lake. She thought he must have been unfaithful to her, and just wanted to forget everything. But he never admitted it. One night she noticed a man walking around her house, it was not for the first time that she'd seen him, but then she saw him again in the daylight and realized that this was an FBI agent.

"What is this? Had the FBI been informed about Holt? Then why...?" I could not get it.

"Not really. Holt must have been suspected by the agent to whom the first wife of Holt had talked. And this had gone nowhere, so many years ago. Now, if she'd invented this agent she might as well say he'd been making inquiries on Holt in his off-duty hours. She could have slept with him so that some people could see him around the house, couldn't she? And later on, getting in bad car accident, the man must have left a few records on Holt. Why not? If Holt had been known to the FBI as a former Russian agent, it would have made no sense. What else is she writing there?" Vlad wondered, scrolling the pages.

The pang of guilt preyed upon Holt's mind, and it seemed not to be through any fault of his own. He probably feared his past was about to catch up with him, he feared they could offer him a job he would not be able to refuse, and she noticed him look over his shoulder a few times... and then he had gone missing. He told her of having AIDS and of his wish to leave for Berlin, to say goodbye to his family and friends. She let him go, but she did not believe him. And he stayed there with that fear of his... In between those letters there were some others, that spoke of the children, the hospital, the mortgage and the sick grandmother, including treatments for stomach ulcers.

It seemed a true work of fiction, all that was missing was a proper book jacket.

"This has already been clear. But now we know they had begun to cover up for Schumann three years back. That's rather a long time. So they must have gotten a witness to reconfirm that Smith had turned into Holt. And not Holt's wife, so there must be someone else."

That time we had no idea it might be someone who was not a mere witness.

CHAPTER NINE

PURE ZERO

In the morning I woke up hearing the echo of lonely steps in the stairway crashing the brick rubble, stump and restless. It was Hoffmann. Vlad peeped into my room, signaling me to jump into my clothes.

"Frau Holt!" I could hear Hoffmann's voice.

"Guten Morgen, Herr Hoffmann. Would you like to come in? Would you like a cup of coffee?" I asked, peeping into the stairwell.

"Yes, thank you. Have I caught you in bed? I'll make you coffee, take your time getting dressed," he suggested as he made his way to the kitchen.

"There must be a mini cake in the fridge," I hinted.

When I entered the kitchen Hoffmann was brewing coffee. Now I could see him much closer. His face still looked rather like a soft snowball, with his bird-like piercing black eyes sunken in the swollen circles; his bloodless lips the same and resembled the under melted snow edge. He took off his hat and coat, he was silver-haired, a blonde with a short haircut. I could see his skin shine through the thinning hair on his forehead.

"Could you read this?" he asked nodding at the newspaper spread on the table, and put the cups of coffee beside it.

I froze with a mini cake in my hand as I noticed the picture of Vlad Holt. It was definitely the man. Indeed, he bore a striking resemblance to Vlad, and Vlad seemed somewhat fragile beside that man. It was a short article telling now they'd found a freezer with the corpse of Vlad Holt, a consulting firm manager, on the East River side. The man had been there for three years. It was no murder. The man had died of a heart attack. As per his wife, he'd come down with AIDS three years ago, and left to say goodbye to his friends in Berlin and to get treatment in a private clinic in Switzerland. He had not wanted anyone to know, so she'd been making it seem like a breakup, with her husband allegedly gone to join his family in Germany. He had not called, so she'd started to believe her husband had left her. This turn of events was a bitter revelation to her.

The article said nothing of her visit to Berlin in connection with the funeral of her husband's ashes, the one deceased less than two weeks ago, who'd had another wife whom he'd only married a year earlier in Tallinn.

"Is this the man you married to a year ago?" Hoffmann asked, placing a cup of coffee right in front of me.

"You can tell me, it's no big deal, they say I look like a priest," he pressed me a little bit.

It flashed into my mind, *Well, if you are a priest, I must be the Pope*, and I responded with,

"No, it's not the man. But he resembles him so much I don't know what to say."

"You've landed in a mess, as you can see... Could you tell me, this Herr Leman, does he look like the man you've married?"

"Herr Leman... looks more like the man I'd be happy to marry."

"There may have been some distinctive features, like a scar, for instance?"

"Oh my god, it's so silly, but I can't remember anything."

"And what about his prick, was it the size you could hold in your fist or bigger? Aren't you able to recollect this much, at least?" he demanded with a slight irritation.

"Bigger. What do you want from me? I never thought to attend to his corpse's identification."

"Well, this should not be your husband, beginning with his prick. You see how easy it turns out for you. In case you recollect something, you may give me a call. And for the time being let us just have some coffee. You should not discuss this with anyone. And don't you tell anyone it had been Herr Leman, okay? You'll find it easy to lie. If someone starts to ask you questions, give me a call. Anyway, don't hesitate to give me a call. It's the process... They are about to make anyone a spy." Hoffmann paused for a second, then had a gulp of coffee as if thinking whether he should tell me or not. "There is something weird about this story. This Vlad Holt is said to have been seen two weeks ago here in Berlin. This is just word of mouth, yet it sounds more trustworthy than the corpse in the freezer. How could it have been possible, if the man had stayed all this time in the freezer? By the way, I've paid a visit to the mother of Herr Leman," Hoffmann gave me a glance, and said, "Herr Leman has a sick mother. Did you know this? Hmm... he must not have been ready to tell you. She's doing fine, she is not really worried about him, and she told me he must have gone on the lam, which sometimes happens." Hoffmann looked around the walls of the kitchen, and then peeped out the window. "Well, if you feel comfortable in these parts, you better stay here."

When he took his leave Hoffmann said he would always be happy to see me and have a cup of tea together.

After seeing the man out, I headed back to the kitchen. Vlad was reading the article, and he could not take his eyes off the photo of Vlad Holt. The resemblance was striking.

"Does Hoffmann think that this woman posing for Holt's wife is actually an agent herself? True, she must be an agent to have remained unbothered by her husband's missing for three years," Vlad snorted, putting the newspaper aside, still unable to take his eyes off the picture. "I never thought I could one day see him like that," he said in contemplation. "Oh gosh, I've already died twice in the past week."

"Does that mean, set to zero? Is this the way you wanted it?" I inquired.

"It's not bad at all, for the moment."

"And if Schumann had been covered by the British, how could they have ruined everything they must have been working on over the years? Who could play for the agent Smith now? Who would be giving testimony in court for Schumann's case?" I wondered.

"No one has ruined anything. This wife of Holt's would make a good witness. She may tell them Holt had been recruited and then lost contact with his curator right after the fall of the Soviet Union. Schumann had been recruited along with him and also remained a sleeper agent. A woman in court would make a more striking picture than a male. Erm, however... well, someone would normally reconfirm her words. There must be a witness we don't know about."

"Oh my goodness, I've been thinking the life of that Holt had been ruined due to a passing similarity with you, but he actually warped his own life himself through this marriage to the agent. Vlad, Hoffmann has been visiting your mother, she's doing fine, and she is not worried about you. Is she an agent?" I meant it a joke, without much thought, but then shot a glance at Vlad and fell dumb with the guess.

Victor told me his curator used to be a very old woman that he loved as a mother, she suffered with bad legs and he used to carry her in his arms. That is why Victor had not been crushed by the red tape of the former Union. She'd left for Argentina to live with his father. Yet... she might have returned. What if she were the one?

Vlad did not answer; he was thinking his own thoughts,

"Hmm, there you go, they must have finally figured out the deal is of higher value than the agent Smith, whoever he might have been. So, there seems to be three different options for the agent Smith: the American Vlad Holt, Andreas Leman and then some other Holt in charge of the deal. Brown just saw the man alive two weeks ago. He could not have been the American Holt. Holt had been kept a long time in the freezer."

"And what could be the explanation?"

I asked this question hopping to finally hear something like, *No idea*. It seemed to me, if I ever asked him, *Vlad, I want sex*, his reply would be, *There, I've got a list of the people you've got to have a sleepover with*.

"If they come to suspect that wife of Holt's, the British would not withhold they'd been keeping this Holt in sight, and the woman was indeed their source. That is why they'd rather say that there had been some tasks for Holt to complete before anyone learned of his death."

"Vlad, I thought you could at least for once reply with: No idea."

"I can. I've never really been able to comprehend this entire fucking British classic."

At nighttime I went out to use the pay phone. It was beastly cold outdoors; I swallowed some icy air and spluttered as if it were alcohol. The shell ice on the pavement glisted like a frozen pond; I lost my footing and stepped on the fringe where my ice-bound crispy footprints crunched like broken glass, resonating with a screechy echo in the depths of the backyard. Victor's voice sounded far away and alien, he said there would be a witness in court, Vlad Holt.

I thought I must have misheard and listened to the same message for another time, and then still missed the point, by making neither heads nor tails of my own thoughts, I went back at a lively pace. The fear I'd experienced when hearing of my husband's death, was back now and winged my steps.

"Vlad, Victor's just told me there will be a witness in court, Vlad Holt. What the fuck does that mean?!"

"That actually means the agent Smith has turned up a live. They may have believed the defector from Boston, the one Victor had been talking to, and the man failed to recognize the agent Smith in Andreas Leman. So just about anyone may go for the agent Smith. And now this guy "Tom, Dick or Harry" has turned up. I wonder if the man could have any resemblance to me. Holy shit, I'm sick and tired of looking at my own self in different versions. Could I just go fuck this one like I fuck myself?"

Like this book?

Maybe you leave a review?

THE GODS SMILE ON THE BASTARDS

Book Three of The Sleeper Series

by Anna Schlegel

ISBN: 9780998185392
ASIN: B06XYVGTK6

Once you are able to see the intelligence's handwriting, you may see the words of failure inscribed in the same handwriting, telling of a failure they are yet unaware of.

In looking at that other man from afar, he found it hard to shake off the feeling of observing his own self from the outside. That other man resembled him way too much. The man was better than him, more experienced, and he looked more convincing, and rather like a slime ball. Everyone could see it. The man succeeded in making everyone believe he was truly him, in person. And the man could prove it.

What could eventually happen if the man slipped away? Then the only guy remaining would be him. And he would be constrained to be more like his former self. For all those long years, he had plain forgotten what kind of a person he was, underneath. He would have to recollect and become somewhat more life-like. He would hardly be able to make it, really, unless he was dead. But then, would that be a preferable option; something they truly wanted?

Why do intelligence people become defectors? There may be two answers. One is obvious. They become defectors due to a landmark case against some other turncoat. Every agent, while keeping a close watch on the case, usually dissected the defendant's mistakes so he thought he would never do anything similar, convinced that he could be smarter, employing a lot more caution...

The second answer is something else. People come to be turncoats long before they start working for the spy directorate. So, read it all: this is worth knowing. This is the answer from a legend. Listen to it, give it a touch, and you'll be blessed with the smile of God.

You may have a wish to learn a bit more on the legendary agent, and these books would most probably catch your eyes. Would you be able to find in them the answer to the question, whether Philby was indeed a legendary spy? I doubt it.

A Spy Among Friends: Kim Philby and the Great Betrayal

by Ben Macintyre, John le Carré

To my mind, it's a better idea to read Phillip Knightley. He starts his book from the point when he stepped across the threshold of Kim Philby's apartment in Moscow. This book has an answer.

Philby: KGB Mastermind

by Phillip Knightley

I'm writing about Kim Philby from a different side, that is from the side where he used to be loved, and where he remains as a living legend.

From Russia with love,

Anna Schlegel

MONEY CAN'T LIE

Book One of The Sleeper Series

by Anna Schlegel

ISBN: 9780998185347
ASIN: B01M1BZR1X

Should there be three pieces of crap this is of the British intelligence classic.

He was not worth a straw to Intelligence; he was a mere sleeper, just a small coin. One day he felt that behind his back there was someone else; someone a big shot of such high value that they could not afford to lose him. Who could that be, - a recent defector? He had no idea.

He could only sense a trace of him, barely-there, just a nip. They were seeking to ward off the trail, and not just by drawing it aside. Now it appeared to lead straight to him. Every little thing pointed to him.

The trace would be lifeless, classically beautiful and as such stone-dead.

ONLY ONE REALITY THAT KILLS

Book Four of The Sleeper Series

by Anna Schlegel

ISBN: 9780999127605

It happens to everyone without exception. It will inevitably happen to you unless you live under the wing of the legend.

He was back. No one believed it was him until he started killing those who had no more doubts.

LIE MAKES ME LIVE
Book Five of The Sleeper Series

by Anna Schlegel

Coming soon

This game of the intelligence, we were either to see through it, or die.

There is an old brain teaser about three different gods, God of Lie, God of Truth and God of Chance. One of them lied all the time, another told everyone the truth only, and the third one could either tell the truth or lie. So who of them was who in there?

Who was that man? There happened to be three people who had told they knew the man. So who of them could be telling the truth? And who must have been lying? Who could have been led up the path? And what kind of person was he himself? He was the only man to know the answer, but he was the God of Lie.

ABOUT THE AUTHOR

Why do I know so much of the Intelligence? It must have come from between the bedsheets, and not just this much. Victor returned to Moscow after a few years of work as a financial expert. He was more of a moneyman than a special service agent, even more he was a swindler. He became a raider like so many others, during those years. He used to have both good luck and failure in bank seizures, in which he lost money. I imperceptibly turned to be just the same like him.

These books are written from an adventurer's perspective. There are no good guys, since those good guys have no chance of attracting a female. Women want bastards.

Why read my books? I've got the undeniable strength of being a Russian author, which means that I'm writing about the Russian Intelligence without using much fiction.

Of course, these are just mere fiction novels, a kind of multi-twist mind game; yet I'm describing events the way they could have touched me in reality. So these books actually represent my "might-have-been" by seizing the fact that I could have lived a number of alternative lives. Understandably, one life is enough for me: my behind would hardly stand more adventures. I'm writing about things that I find interesting. I've only read a few books of spy fiction - for the most part, they are deadly boring.

I was born in Moscow. I studied at the Moscow State University at the Philosophical facility. I got a PhD in philosophy and stayed without work and without money. The financial crisis began. Some years I looked for a work, but took it easy. I became a securities trader in an investment company by chance. And then came the default in 1998. I was without work again.

This was my best time. I became the financial middleman for off-market private transactions. I had nothing. I had been looking for too-big deals. But then there was a time when it was quite possible for me to be the middleman in the sale of a Libyan oil tanker or for the sale of an aircraft abroad. I got sick of conducting multi-million dollar transactions and lost all sense of reality.

I met Victor. Capturing the bank was in my sights. The insider of the bank was its vice-president. I write about his capture almost verbatim. Before leaving, he gave me his three passports... So I do not know his real name. There were no closed doors for him. He had friends from the federal agency for government communication and information from the board of directors of Deutsche Bank. All kinds of people.

Years passed. Victor is long gone. And there are fewer middlemen.

I feel myself to be on the way out. My whole generation is on the way out as well; those who are described as robbing the country.

I like those who robbed the country, and I'm pleased about how it was done. They were really talented financiers; nothing worse than the financiers on Wall Street. They left the country and took the money with them.

Since then, Moscow's air did not smell of millions any longer. But, it seemed to me, it was still in the depths of my house between a pile of white shirts. Now there are no more financial middlemen. The young have gotten jobs first. They receive a salary at the end of the month, and seem to have already forgotten the smell of crazy millions.

It's like being drunk. There's a dizziness from it ... They did not want to breathe this air. They did not want to poison their lives. They earned their money. They had wives, children, dogs, and cars, which it was necessary to care of... Their heads have overflowed with thoughts of petty cash.

Then the middlemen were old. And I stayed with them. Therefore, the heroes of my novels are in their sixties. To the former friends who stayed in the stock market, I became infected. No, I just died. And I smell of sweet cadaveric decay. It seemed to me that I was among the dead. And it felt really bad for me, as a living being. But I shared their way of thinking. I was the same as they were: ridiculous and old-fashioned, useless clutter, rubbish. Market garbage. My friends were precisely the same as middle-aged gentlemen.

Sometimes I catch a strange look directed towards me, but then forget about it. The metropolis wiped me from their memory. There was no need to be as nice as kind people who talk with clients and colleagues daily. I had a different way of talking. My talking always led to a deal. And if it didn't, I would give the finger and immediately forget the useless person, as if shaking off dust. And that's all.

I have nothing to regret. I had nothing to blame myself for. Dogs wouldn't blame themselves for their dog's life, would they?

I cannot return to the stock market. It has changed. Brokers, buyers, and sellers have been changed. They all grew up a little. They have got each other for 0.1 percent interest, ready to sell their ass to everyone at 0.5 percent, and would sell their own mother at one percent. I could not do that. The market has kicked me out as garbage.

And the old, among whom I used to be, are gone. The reality of small money has burned out people all around me as fire burns wood. Sometimes it seems to me that I have gone mad; that I live in a world turned inside out. Sometimes I would like to be like anyone... to have a rest, eat, dress, buy a car...

But I can't do it. It would be a living death.

It seems to me I would lose days and years and would end up in devastation and poverty. And I would lose the scent of money, and my skills ... so I clung to the sale of oil, diamonds, and bank guarantees, though I'm sure that it was simply thin air and there was nothing behind it. Sometimes I woke up and thought that all was not with me. But I lived and breathed the air of millions. It was my life. In my life, I gained money from thin air. Emptiness is a magnet for me.

Now I have got nothing. I do not care. I like my life. I like to go for millions. It's impossible to stop me. I might have to be put down like a mad dog.

And I still have a sense of money. I can smell the street's air and say that the market has changed. It smells as sharp as the smell of fresh bread from a bakery in the winter.

THE DEAD BANK DIARY SERIES

THE DEAD BANK DIARY
Book One of The Dead Bank Diary Series
ISBN: 9780986174919
ASIN: B00OPAZQMI

FOR THOSE IN THE SHADE
Book Two of The Dead Bank Diary Series
ISBN: 9780986174964
ASIN: B014Q92DE6

THE PRINTS ON THE SNOWS OF YESTERYEAR
Book Three of The Dead Bank Diary Series
ISBN: 9780986174988
ASIN: B017KYY2MA

SOME DAY I'LL HIT A BANK
Book Four of The Dead Bank Diary Series
ISBN: 9780998185323
ASIN: B01LYZ3XQX

THE FROZEN DEBT
Book Five of The Dead Bank Diary Series
ISBN: 9780998185309
ASIN: B01LX1AKZ7

MY GOD IS MONEY
Book Six of The Dead Bank Diary Series
Coming Soon

AUTHOR'S NOTE

In these books there are no cops, no killings. There is much about the illegal takeover of banks, and a powerful amount of money. I know how to pump up a bank, and how to bankrupt a bank. I love beautiful gray schemes on the verge of being crimes. My stories are about fraud through the eyes of a swindler. There are no good guys.

I write about the golden-time bankers, from 1998, when neither the police nor the intelligence services, or any crimes haven't prevented the banks from making money.

These novels are not based on a true story, but you will face this reality in every word.

ABOUT THE DEAD BANK DIARY SERIES

These are stories about a man who is not alive anymore. He was a financier, a retired intelligence officer. I had the good luck to arrange a couple of financial frauds. We bumped into each other before the recession, in the flood of shit, together in the dust.

After his death I still had the power of attorney.

Of course, Victor knew I wouldn't be able to work on his contacts. I had tried. Now it's funny to think of it. I am, and always have been, a go-between, a rat. Nobody needs middlemen. They get rid of them; they send them to Hell. But I had a white shirt with a necktie, and copies of million dollar contracts for oil, gas, diamonds, and rare-earth metals: light as air, rolled fax sheets with lots of zeroes. They made me giddy; they made me drunk. And I ran along with them, and easily foisted them onto the middlemen: muddy, middle-aged misters.

When some of the first deals failed, I went into hysterics. I wanted to throw everything in.

Once I had a dream. In my dream, I heard a telephone call,

"Miss Schlegel? We need your signature to extend a contract concluded by Mr..."

I woke up scared; something turned over inside of me. I realized that I was spending my life waiting for such a call. It didn't matter where it caught me.

But there was no going back. Once you've taken a step forward, you realize you can't turn back anymore.

Why did he leave all this to me? I looked over the papers, recalling past years, deals, people, talks: everything from the first meeting to the last minute. And I couldn't find anything for me; because it wasn't for me, actually, but for the old me. So I changed. I became a con.

My life was changed. Sometimes it was as convincing and disgusting as the life of a whore. It was as inaccessible as the man who despises you. It was like vomit or sweat from the body from a heavy hangover's shivers. You wish to run, but there's no place to run to. It's a cold stupor. So it's stupid to look at the smeared corpse on the road, and it's impossible to regain consciousness to look away. This passion nests in the heart, and you don't know what it is.

I have his photo, the last one, taken at Arkhangelskoe hospital. Summer. We're sitting on the edge of a dried-up fountain. He embraces me with one arm, and I'm lost next to him. He is gray-haired and corpulent. He has a mocking look. And behind us there are towering white marble angels.

THE DEAD BANK DIARY

Book One of The Dead Bank Diary Series

by Anna Schlegel

ISBN: 9780986174919
ASIN: B00OPAZQMI

———————————————————

The rats living on the refuse of the bank's backyard stay full at all time

This is not a robbery. A bank is taken with all its guts: accounts, debts, points of exchange, the staff to the last secretary, the building. This is beautiful and clean fraud.

I was out of work, while all around you could smell millions, even in the air outside. It was an unforgettable smell of public debt, oilfields, gold, bank guarantees, diamonds... I wanted to breathe in the air of easy cash Moscow, to revel and roll in this air. I could feel the smell of money in the wind on my face. This air was used to make up funds overnight, to make a fortune, to go to rack and ruin and then grow rich again. It was blowing freely across the wreckage of the sold-out Soviet empire.

I was asked to help redeem the debts of a bank. The insider man at the bank held the post of Vice President.

A bit of danger and a bit of love.

FOR THOSE IN THE SHADE

Book Two of The Dead Bank Diary Series

by Anna Schlegel

ISBN: 9780986174964
ASIN: B014Q92DE6

You may live your whole life without getting to know who you are, and sometimes this is for the better

It was a bank robbery, however this time the gunmen came not for the cash but for the bank itself, and all that followed happened faster than a domino knockdown.

The bank was bankrupted professionally.

Bad debts of the Third World countries, Cuba, Zimbabwe, Morocco, and The Congo have been returned on the bank's balance sheet. Once, the bank sold the debts to itself, to an offshore company.

Who did this?

The banker finds out the bank in Amsterdam... and has taken it over completely.

THE PRINTS ON THE SNOWS OF YESTERYEAR

Book Three **of** The Dead Bank Diary Series

by Anna Schlegel

ISBN: 9780986174988
ASIN: B017KYY2MA

The best one to rob the bank is the banker himself

The bank, facing bankruptcy, fell out of the hands like a snowball rolling downhill to flattening everything under its weight.

Behind every bankruptcy there are people who make it happen. But there are no influential people. Big figures are absent. It seems you stay face to face with the emptiness.

This happens when the Central Bank is playing against you.

SOME DAY I'LL HIT A BANK

Book Four of The Dead Bank Diary Series

by Anna Schlegel

ISBN: 9780998185323
ASIN: B01LYZ3XQX

The bomb lives to its internal time

My life became lonely and monotonous, almost mechanical in nature, with a mechanism akin to a ticking bomb. It could be ticking for days and weeks, quiet and imperceptible, to blow up everything around at the right time.

This is the way common folks used to live in the past, bakers and shoemakers. They lived their lives until the revolution burst out. It was their time. And then they went out the door of their bakery and shoe shop for good to take the ministry chairs and cut the heads off the aristocracy, by weaving plots and intrigues. I knew I would not miss my time.

It seemed to me I could go on for another ten years, only to one day stumble on a terse line in the newspaper and realize: my time has come.

THE FROZEN DEBT

Book Five of The Dead Bank Diary Series

by Anna Schlegel

ISBN: 9780998185309
ASIN: B01LX1AKZ7

When totally nude have a look, maybe you still have the shoulder loops

One morning he stayed bare-ass, there was no money, no name, no wife, and nothing left... just his shoulder loops.

The deal Victor had set up six years ago kept running like clockwork and suddenly came to a halt. The accounts of the company formerly owned by Victor were blocked by the public prosecution. The man who found Victor in Moscow offered to give him everything back, his company and his board membership and... his wife.

Upon his arrival in Berlin Victor realized that all parties wanted a goner.

And Victor was an ideal goner, as he was also a mole.

Anna Schlegel has a degree in philosophy. She was Securities trader before the recession. The last ten years she has been involved in off-market private transactions as a middleman in Moscow.

Anna lives in Novi Sad, Serbia.

CONTACTS INFORMATION

For information about the author, please visit
TheSleeper.club
thedeadbankdiary@gmail.com

For information about the published books, please contact
Schlegel Press Association at
schlegelpressassociation@gmail.com